N

Rimrock

CLIFFS

Big Cave

Cave Bear

CLAN
CAMPSITE

VALLEY

Cave Lion

OAK
FOREST

Red
Deer

wamp

Hyena

SPRUCE
FOREST

LAND
OF THE
PAINTED
CAVE

Boar

Ibex

River

© 1988 Anita Karl

BOY OF THE PAINTED CAVE

JUSTIN DENZEL

PHILOMEL BOOKS
NEW YORK

▪ I owe a debt of gratitude to the scientists, historians and photographers who, interested in the prehistoric world of Altamira and other southern European cave communities, painstakingly collected specimens and other research which resulted in a body of work that helped re-create that ancient world.

I have received help from many people but none more so than my editor, Patricia Lee Gauch, at Philomel Books. She spent long hours carefully going over each revision, suggesting vital changes and additions, deleting superfluous prose, weeding out clichés, refusing to settle for anything but the very best.

I am also indebted to my son and daughter-in-law, Ken and Elsie Denzel, who initiated me into the world of word processing, making the difficult task of revision almost a pleasure.

Finally I wish to thank Josephine, my wife, who spent many evenings going over the rough drafts, correcting my wayward spelling and unique style of punctuation. Without her patient efforts and moral support this book may not have been written.

Book design by Gunta Alexander.
Map illustration by Anita Karl.
Printed in the United States.

Library of Congress Cataloging-in-Publication Data
Denzell, Justin F. Boy of the painted cave / by Justin Den-
zel. p.   cm. Summary: Forbidden to make images, fourteen-
year-old Tao, the boy with the bad foot, yearns to be a cave
painter, recording the figures of the mammals, rhinos,
bison, and other animals of his prehistoric times.
ISBN 0-399-21559-X   [I. Cave drawings—Fiction.
2. Man, Prehistoric—Fiction.] I. Title.   PZ7.D4377Cav
1988   [Fic]—dc19   87-36609   CIP AC

20 19 18 17 16 15 14 13 12 11

• AUTHOR'S NOTE •

Eighteen to twenty thousand years ago in the Dordogne valley of Southern France and around the foothills of the Pyrenees mountains, in Spain, there lived a Stone Age people who hunted the ancient beasts, the mammoths, the horses and woolly rhinos, the giant oxen and bison.

All over the world other people did much the same thing. But only here, in this small corner of Europe, did there arise a group of superb artists who adorned the walls of their caves with beautiful paintings of those magnificent animals.

Most of the primitive beasts are gone now, many of them extinct, a few domesticated and kept alive by man. But their colorful images live on, in the hidden caverns of the early cave painters.

This is the story of a young cave boy who dreamed of becoming such a cave painter. It tells of his fascination with the wild creatures around him and of his fight against superstition and taboos.

It tells of a world that has long since gone, a world that we will never see again.

*This book is for my
grandchildren
Megan, Stephanie and Christopher
with much love.*

BOY OF THE PAINTED CAVE

■ ONE

Tao looked out across the valley with its endless waves of yellow grass rippling under the late afternoon sun. He could see the small band of hunters walking ahead, turning over logs and stones, searching for ground squirrels, moles and grubs.

Dirt matted their dark beards, burrs and stickers clung to their bearskin robes. They had been out three days, but the hunting was not good. Now they were returning home, tired, almost empty-handed.

The boy watched as the hunters disappeared over the brow of the hill. All day Tao had waited for this moment. With a rabbit in his hand and a leather pouch filled with moles and field mice dangling from his belt, he quickly hobbled over to the foot of a high embankment, where a smooth expanse of white sand had been washed down by the melting snows.

He looked around once again, took a deep breath

and placed the rabbit on the ground. Then, with the point of his spear, he began tracing the shape of the rabbit in the sand.

He worked hurriedly, starting with the head, running the spear around the ears and along the back and stubby tail. When he came to the legs, his hand slipped, causing the spear to gouge a hole in the sand. He broke off a nearby willow branch and brushed away the drawing, then started over again. This time he worked carefully, guiding the spear along the natural curves of the animal's body. When it was finished, he stepped back, studying it for a moment. He shook his head. No, it did not look like a rabbit. It was too stiff, not real.

He felt a flush of anger and he shoved the rabbit aside. He looked over his shoulder again to be sure he was alone, then knelt down on the sand. With the fingers of his right hand he began to draw a picture of a bear. This he was sure he could do. Working from memory, he drew the huge head with its open mouth, showing the row of sharp teeth, the small round ears and the short snout.

As he worked, a warm feeling welled up in him. He forgot the hunters and the rabbit. He thought only of the big brown bears he had seen digging for roots in the marsh grass or scooping salmon out of the icy creeks down in the valley. He remembered their strong shoulders and shaggy brown coats, and for a moment the image became a living beast flowing from his mind, through his hand, directly onto the sand.

He finished his drawing by sketching in the high-arched back and sturdy legs. Then he stood up, brushing the sand from his knees. He looked down at the drawing, smiling broadly. It was good, he thought, the best he had ever done. Yet with time and practice he knew he could do better.

He did not remember when he first began making pictures. It must have been many summers ago when he lived with Kala. At first she was frightened of this. It was taboo and she tried to stop him. Then she let him go. But he could draw only on the dirt floor within the skin hut, where he would not be seen.

Suddenly his thoughts were interrupted by a soft rustling sound. With a shuffling of his deerskin boots he stamped out the picture and dropped quietly into a patch of tall grass. He waited, his heart pounding. He knew he could be severely punished, even banished, if he were caught making images. Except for a chosen few it was a strong taboo and against the secret rites of the clan.

Yet he longed to be an image maker, to be a cave painter like old Graybeard. He knew it was a foolish hope, for he was born of no shaman, he was the son of no chief or leader. He was only Tao, the boy with the bad foot. He did not even know his own father. His mother had died long before he could remember, and there was no elder to help him. Because of this, and because of his bad foot, he knew he could never become a Chosen One.

Whenever he saw the bison out on the plains, or

the giant aurochs and cave lions, he wanted to paint their pictures on the walls of the Secret Cavern, a magic place, far back in Big Cave, where only the Chosen Ones could go.

Often, at night, he lay in front of Kala's hut listening to the crackling fire and looking up at the sky. He saw pictures of deer and horses amongst the stars. By day the billowing clouds became herds of antelope or the lumbering shapes of the mountains-that-walk, the mammoths.

Always during the hunts, he lagged behind the other hunters to watch the giant vultures tracing lazy circles beneath the clouds or to catch a glimpse of a woolly rhino outlined against the horizon. Sometimes seeing these things made him light-headed, almost bursting with joy, and he wanted others to see them as he did.

He knew that Garth and the other hunters did not understand this. Even Volt, the leader, looked upon him as an idler and a dreamer, unworthy of respect or manhood. He liked Garth best of all, because sometimes the big black-bearded man tried to help him. But when the other hunters came by, Garth often turned away and had other things to do.

Once again Tao heard the soft rustling sound in the grass. He waited, afraid to move. Then slowly he crept toward the sound, searching through the grass until he found a trail of pugmarks going around in circles. He gripped his spear tighter and fingered the leather pouch hanging from his belt. He was sure the scent of the dead mice had attracted a hungry animal and he had an uneasy feeling that he was being watched.

He waited silently, listening. Off in the distance he heard the harsh, scolding caw of a raven. That was all. He started walking again, along the foot of the cliffs, heading back for camp. He had only gone a few paces when the rustling noise came again.

This time he turned quickly, ready to defend himself. Then he saw it, peering at him through the shadows, a young wolf, its slitted eyes low and threatening.

Tao hunched down and raised his spear. If it was only one wolf it would be an easy target. He started to throw. Then he noticed the animal swaying back and forth on unsteady legs. Weak and half starved, its ribs showed through the scraggly patches of gray hair. Its yellow eyes looked up at Tao with a vacant stare. It was only half grown and Tao was sure it must have been deserted by the pack.

Slowly the boy lowered his spear. He could not bring himself to kill this helpless animal. Besides, such a scrawny beast would be a poor prize to take back to the clan.

Tao put out his hand, speaking softly to the frightened animal. "Come," he said, "I mean you no harm. You are hungry and I have food." He held up one of the dead field mice. But the young wolf backed away, a faint snarl curled on its lips, saliva dripping from its mouth. Tao slit the mouse open with his flint knife and dangled it in front of the wolf. Again the animal cringed and shied away, its thin legs trembling.

"Here," said Tao, "eat. You are hungry. Do not be afraid." With careful aim he tossed the mouse on the ground in front of the wolf.

The little animal came closer, slowly, one step at a time, its yellow eyes watching the boy intently. It nuzzled the dead mouse, pushing it around, licking at the oozing fluids. Yet it still refused to eat. Tao shook his head, puzzled.

It was growing dark now and he had to get back to the clan people with the rest of the field mice. He felt badly about leaving the little wolf, but he could not take him with him. He left the gutted mouse lying near the wolf's muzzle.

As he started to back away, the little animal looked up at him with pleading eyes. Tao shook his head sadly but there was little more he could do.

He made his way between the huge boulders that littered the foot of the cliffs. Born with a bad right foot, a foot that bent down and turned in slightly, Tao walked with a limp. However, by curling his foot around the shaft of his spear, he had learned to travel with greater ease and, when in a hurry, he could vault over the hills faster than a running man. Now, because of the darkness, he went slowly, picking his way through the weaving shadows.

He continued on through the oakwood forest until the fires of the little camp came into view. Here, in the clearing, a small group of skin huts was set up under the shelter of a massive rock overhang jutting out from the limestone cliffs. High above, Tao could see the great fire of the Endless Flame burning brightly, lighting up the entrance to Big Cave.

A white haze of smoke filled the clearing and flickering campfires lit up the darkness. Tao smelled the odor of cooking meat. Fat dropped from the spits, sizzling on the hot coals as the women grunted to each other and roasted the few ground squirrels and moles the hunters had brought back. Children sat on their haunches in front of the huts. They had been many months with little food, and their sunken eyes looked up at Tao. He knew his handful of field mice would not go far to ease their hunger.

He glanced quickly at Volt's bearskin hut in the center of the camp, hoping the big leader would not see him. Then he went directly to the edge of the clearing where two bison skin robes were lashed securely to a frame of cross poles, forming a ragged hut. He knelt down in front of it and called softly, "Kala."

The flap opened and an old woman peered out. Her square face was lined with wrinkles. Strings of gray hair hung down over her eyes, and she held a child in her arms. She smiled broadly, her big teeth yellow from chewing deer hide and spruce gum. "You are late," she said. "But you are safe."

Tao nodded and held out two of the mice. "We traveled far," he said. "But we did not get much."

The woman took the mice in her brawny hand and held them up by the tails. "I still have some dried grubs," she said, "and some roots. With these I can make a meal for the little one."

The little one was a girl child, an orphan from the winter famine. If it had not been for Kala, the elders would have taken her up among the boulders and left her for the hyenas. By caring for her, she had saved the child's life, much as she had done for Tao.

"Now you have another," said Tao, smiling, touching the old woman's shoulder.

The woman thought for a moment. "Three so far," she said. "You were the first."

Tao remembered it well. She had raised him as her own, when others had turned their backs because of his bad foot. He stayed with her for twelve summers, learning much from her wisdom and kindness.

"The sun is getting warmer," said Tao. "Soon the hunting will be good and there will be enough to eat." He said it even though he feared it might not be true. Perhaps Graybeard would come and paint images in the Secret Cavern. If the spirits were pleased, great herds of horses, deer and bison would fill the plains and forests. The people would eat well and the clan would thrive. There would be many pelts with which to make new robes and boots, ivory and antlers to make needles, spears and knives.

Kala and Tao talked for a few more minutes. Then the woman listened and put her finger to her lips.

"Go," she whispered, "before Volt comes." She went back into the hut and closed the flap, and for a moment Tao could hear her humming to the little one as she started the meal.

Tao went to the center of the camp near the large fire, to turn over the rest of his field mice. He was almost there when a dark shadow fell across his path. It was Volt, the leader. The big man planted himself in front of the boy. His sheepskin robe was singed and stained with spots of blackberry. He wore a necklace of bear claws. His dark beard was wild and unkempt.

Tao felt a sinking feeling in the pit of his stomach, but he stood firm. In the light of the fire he saw the man's left cheek gashed with livid scars that always turned his face into an ugly scowl.

The man pointed a fat, hairy finger at the boy and grunted. "Where have you been?"

Tao hesitated, at first not knowing what to say. "I stopped by the meadow."

The big man grumbled. "You are always late, always behind the others, dreaming, wasting time. You are a poor hunter when the people are hungry."

Tao saw the other hunters gathering around, attracted by the harsh words. Good, thought Tao, now he would tell them about the wolf dog. Wolf dogs were taboo, but he didn't have to tell them he tried to feed it. Maybe the others would listen. "I heard a noise in the high grass," said the boy eagerly. "I wondered what it was and I thought—"

Volt shook his head and interrupted gruffly, "Enough!" he shouted. "We do not need wondering, we do not need thinking or dreaming. *We need food.*"

The heat of anger flushed in Tao's cheeks. This man was like a mountain. He would listen to nothing. His words were always harsh and sullen. He would tell him no more. He handed Volt the pouchful of field mice.

The big man grunted again, glaring down at the boy. "And where is the rabbit?"

Tao's body stiffened. He had forgotten the rabbit.

Volt stepped closer, his eyes narrowing. "You ate the rabbit?"

The other hunters crowded around the boy.

"You ate the rabbit?" Volt repeated, his voice taut.

Tao shook his head, unable to speak. Garth, the black-bearded one, who was always with Volt, knocked him to the ground. Tao lay there in the firelight, looking up at the tight ring of spears.

"No," said Tao, trying to catch his breath. "I would not eat while others are hungry."

Volt brushed the back of his hand across his scarred cheek. "Then where is the rabbit?"

Tao squirmed, the sharp stones pressing against his shoulders. "I . . . I forgot the rabbit. I left it back in the meadow."

Garth looked down at him, frowning, shaking his head.

The men with the spears moved closer, Garth's shadow falling across Tao's face. He saw the dark anger in their eyes.

Volt pushed them aside. "Wait," he said, "there is a better way." He pointed off into the darkness where the tops of the oak trees were black against the purple night. "Go," he ordered, a sneering grin spreading across his face. "You say the rabbit is in the meadow. Go then, find your rabbit in the meadow and do not come back until you do. Maybe then you will learn to keep your mind on the hunting."

Tao got to his feet slowly, brushing himself off. He felt a bitter surge of anger, anger at himself for his own carelessness, anger at these men who would not listen. As he walked out of the camp he saw one of the clan women reach into the fire and pull out a flaming willow torch. She handed it to him and, in the light, Tao saw that it was Kala. He wanted to speak, but she nodded slightly, her deep green eyes warning him to be quiet.

Slowly Tao made his way through the oak forest until he came to the foot of the cliffs bordering the grasslands. He held his torch high, limping across the dried-out streambed and around the scattered boulders.

Once or twice he was sure he heard something moving in the grass, but when he turned around all he saw was the dancing shadows of the stunted willow trees.

He was tired now and hunger gnawed at him. But first he had to find the rabbit. He followed the cliff until he came to the meadow, then looked around for the patch of sand. In the eery light of his torch, the

darkness closed in and everything looked the same—
the rocks, the bushes, the clumps of grass.

Finally he found the sand patch and the scuffed-
out drawings he had made that afternoon. He poked
his spear around in the torchlight and his heart
sank. The rabbit was gone. In its place were the pugmarks of a large hyena.

Now he knew he could not go back to camp, not
tonight, maybe not tomorrow, not until he had
found another rabbit.

■ TWO

Tao propped his torch against a stone, then gathered armfuls of brushwood and kindling and piled them up near the sandy embankment. He set them afire and threw on more sticks and logs until the yellow tongues of flame licked high into the darkness.

Except for a few grubs and a handful of dried berries, he had not eaten since early morning, and he felt a dull emptiness in his stomach. Holding his torch high, he searched about under a group of oak trees, looking for acorns. But it was late in the season and the ground had already been picked over by marmots and pigs.

Just then the gliding shadow of a flying squirrel swooped down from an old dead willow at the top of the embankment. Tao looked up and saw a hole in the scarred white trunk and he knew where he might find a meal. Broken limbs jutted out from the old tree, and it was an easy climb.

Tao reached into the hole, his fingers groping through the warm nest of leaves and fluff. He brought out handfuls of acorns. Back on the ground, he sat on his heels and cracked them open with a handy stone and picked out the bits of meat with his fingertips. The acorns were dry and tasteless, but they helped to take the edge off his hunger. Next he gathered bunches of dried meadowgrass and spread them out on the sand to make a bed. With the embankment at his back and the warm fire in front, he felt safe from the hyenas and prowling leopards.

The night air was cool and still. He lay back on his bed of straw, feeling the prickling stems against his back and smelling the sweet odor of the new grass. Except for the short coughing roar of a cave lion far out in the valley and the hiss and sputter of the fire, the night was quiet.

For a long while he lay awake thinking about his quarrel with Volt and the others over the missing rabbit. The punishment did not bother him, for he had been out alone in the bush many times before and he was not afraid.

At times like this he often thought of his mother, whom he had never seen, and he wondered what she was like. He closed his eyes and saw a picture of a young girl, with hair the color of honey and a round smiling face. He reached out as if to touch her, then withdrew his hand. It was only a vision. He wished he could draw her as he imagined her to be, but this would be taboo. Most of all, it was against the laws of the clan to make an image of a person. It would offend the evil spirits.

Tao shook his head as he huddled down in the loose straw. Why are all these things bad? he wondered. Why is it wrong to draw in the sand, to make a picture on a stone, to be born with a lame foot? Is there nothing good, nothing right? Is this why Volt is always angry? Everything he sees is bad. Kala said she has never seen an evil spirit. If they are real, where do they stay, where do they hide? In the forest, behind the mountains and boulders?

Just then Tao heard a movement in the tall grass. He jumped up quickly and pulled a flaming torch from the fire. As he looked into the darkness he saw only the moving shadows of the stunted willows. Then, just outside of the glare of his torch, he made out a pair of gleaming eyes. Tao froze and gripped his spear tighter. It could be a prowling cave lion or a leopard. If it was bold enough to come within the light of the fire, he would have little chance.

He watched cautiously, waiting for the beast to show itself. Slowly he lifted his spear, ready to throw as the yellow eyes came closer. Then he stopped. Fear left him as he made out the thin gray shape of the little wolf.

The animal cringed and crept up through the grass. Little by little it came into the light of the fire, whining softly. Tao leaned down, clicking his tongue. The animal seemed to be begging for help.

He had heard about wolf dogs before, that some-

times during bad seasons when they are hungry and
half starved they hang about the camps looking for a
bone or a scrap of meat, or to lick at the hearth rocks
where the fat drips. This one was young and thin as
a shadow. If it didn't find something to eat soon it
would die.

Tao squatted down, talking to the animal softly.
"You come back when I have nothing to give you, no
food, no meat."

The wolf remained silent, watching Tao intently.

"You must learn to hunt on your own," said Tao,
creeping closer but still not touching the animal.
"There is food in the fields and in the woods, voles
and mice under the grass, ground squirrels in the
meadow. You must sniff them out and catch them."

The sound of Tao's voice seemed to quiet the animal. It whimpered softly and began to creep up on
its belly until its coal-black nose was only an arm's
length away. Tao reached out to touch the soft muzzle, but the animal pulled back and bared its fangs.
The boy tried again. Once again the young wolf
shied away and would not allow itself to be touched.

Tao sat still, watching, as the animal edged closer.
The wolf dog's ears were laid back, its ribs showed
through the ragged gray fur. Tao saw the hunger in
the yellow eyes. He saw it in the lean face and in the
pale tongue that darted out to lick the thin lips.

Then, in the flickering light of the fire, Tao saw
something else, something glistening white sticking
out of the wolf's mouth. It was not a fang, not a flash

of white tooth, but a long sliver of bone jammed deeply into its upper jaw.

Now Tao understood why the animal refused to eat, why it was so thin and weak. Somehow, in fighting for its food, in pulling or tugging on a piece of meat, a splinter of bone had become lodged in its jaw. Now it could not feed. It could not even hunt.

Tao crept closer, inching nearer and nearer, reaching out slowly, his hand almost touching the wolf's muzzle. The little animal did not move. Its yellow eyes caught the firelight and again its lips pulled back in a low snarl. Tao waited, his heart beating fast. Then, with a sudden lunge, he sprang forward and grasped the wolf's head with one hand and the splinter of bone between the fingers of his other hand.

The little animal jumped back, yelping and crying. But Tao hung on. Boy and wolf twisted and turned, tumbling across the sandbank. The wolf shook his head, violently opening and closing his jaws, trying to escape. Still Tao held on tight, floundering across the sand as the wolf continued to yelp and thrash about. Suddenly the sliver of bone came loose in Tao's fingers. The wolf was free. He ran about in circles, whining, rubbing his bloody muzzle in the damp earth.

"Be quiet," said the boy. He held up the long splinter of bone, blood-smeared, glistening red in the firelight. "Your demon of pain is gone. Now you can eat again."

The wolf dog picked himself up, weaving back and forth on unsteady legs. For a long moment he stared at Tao, his yellow slitted eyes shining, his pink tongue licking at the bleeding wound.

"Go," said Tao. "Go back to your pack and hunt with your friends. You will soon grow strong again."

The little wolf hesitated. Tao saw it look back once or twice. There was a soft rustling of grass as the animal disappeared into the night.

Tao smiled, but after the wolf dog was gone he felt a sense of emptiness. He was alone again.

He got up and threw more dried willow branches and a log of birch wood on the fire, enough to last through most of the night. Then he lay down again. He heard the whooping laugh of the hyenas far out on the grassland and he knew they were hungry too. His hand reached out and his fingers closed around the spear lying beside him. He was tired and there was a weariness in his bones and he fell asleep quickly.

As he slept, Tao drifted off into a narrow tunnel that led into a large cave. On the floor were shells and hollow stones filled with black, yellow and red paints. The walls were smooth and unmarked, waiting for the hand of the painter.

Tao picked up the red shell and dipped his finger into the oily color. With wild sweeps of his hand he began to paint. His arm moved beyond his control as if it had a mind of its own. Slowly a bounding red deer took shape, its antlers thrown back, its nostril flaring as it ran. It leaped over the ground, fear and panic showing in its eyes. Tao put down the red shell and picked up the black one. Once more he dipped his fingers in the paint and began to draw. This time a huge black wolf came forth, racing after the deer. With bounding leaps it gave chase. Great ruffles of fur stood out around its neck and shoulders and a long, waving tail flew out behind it.

Finally Tao picked up the shell containing the yellow paint. He dabbed it on the wall and suddenly the wolf stared out at him with golden eyes. Tao went on drawing and painting, covering the walls with herds of bison and mammoths, horses and au-rochs.

When he awoke, the sun was coming up over the horizon, the fire was a gray heap of smoldering em-bers, and the shrill *kee-kee-kee* of a kestrel came from the branches of the dead willow tree. He rubbed his eyes and glanced around and he knew he had been dreaming.

He stood up and looked out across the grasslands. The valley was bathed in a golden glow of color. The mountains in the distance were morning green. Here and there small patches of snow marked the last footprints of fading winter. Behind him was the long ridge of limestone cliffs, and on top of that were the flatlands, the high plains.

He felt the pangs of early-morning hunger and he started out across the valley through the knee-high grass. He stopped frequently to turn over stones and pull up sod in search of ants and grubs. He was used to going long hours without eating, but now he had gone almost two days without food and he was growing weak. He found a few white grubs and plopped them into his mouth, swallowing them whole. He knew they would taste better roasted, but he could not wait.

Even this was not enough. He would have to find something more. And he knew that if he wanted to go back to camp he would have to catch another rabbit. Once through the grassland he made his way along the edge of the swamp until he came to a thicket of alders and brier bushes. It was dense and tangled with creepers and thorns. He had never been past this place, but beyond, he knew, lay a dark marshland of winding creeks and green forests. The clan people called it the Slough. The elders said it was peopled by demons. The hunters never went there and the women would not dig its roots or harvest its berries lest they become cursed by the evil spirits.

Tao stood on the edge of this forsaken place and thought of the game and food that might lay within. For a moment the threat of taboo held him back. He limped slowly along the edge, undecided, trying to see beyond the tangle of vines and branches. Then, through the thicket, he heard the grunt of a sow and the answering squeal of piglets. He forgot about demons and evil spirits and pushed his way through the thick briers. Heedless of the thorns that scratched his arms and caught at his deerskin leggings, he plunged deeper. Soon the earth became soft and black, and he smelled the musty dampness of the sluggish creeks and heard the rattling call of kingfishers. The dank woodland was dark and green, with shafts of sunlight filtering through the bare branches of the old hornbeams and willows.

Tao stopped and glanced around, wondering if the hand of an evil spirit would strike him. But nothing happened. This place looked no more evil or dangerous than many places he had seen before. Gripping his spear tighter, he went deeper. He came to a shallow stream covered with rafts of new watercress. He scooped some up in his fingers and smelled its freshness. He chewed some and found it crisp and sweet. Oyster mushrooms grew in thick clusters on the trunks of dead birch trees, and berry bushes formed dense thickets between the scrub. The mushrooms were shriveled now and the berries were sparse and dry, but he marked the spot in his mind. By late spring the mushrooms would be lush and the berries would be ripe for picking. In another stream he found a bed of freshwater mussels. He lay on his stomach and reached into the icy water and picked some of them out of the mud. With his flint knife he pried them open and ate the soft pink flesh. He was still hungry, but he felt better now and a new lightness welled up within him. Here was food in abundance. He leaned down and tried to catch a lazy suckerfish that was swimming along the muddy bottom of the stream, almost within his grasp.

Suddenly a hideous shriek echoed through the

marshland. *Wa-woo-oong-eewoo-oo-wahoo,* it went, sending an icy chill racing up Tao's spine. It came from the far side of the creek. Tao jumped up quickly and stood in frozen silence. He looked across the stream to the clump of dark cedars from where the awful scream had come. If he had never seen an evil spirit before, he thought he was about to see one now.

▪ THREE

Tao found a narrow spot along the stream and vaulted across. Picking his way carefully, he crept forward, step by step. He had not gone far when the fiendish scream came again. It was followed by a series of long, hissing sounds and sobbing moans.

For a moment Tao hesitated, uncertain, his heart pounding. Maybe the clan people were right. Maybe there were demons and evil things in this shadowy place after all. If there were, he wondered, did he really want to see them? He waited, trying to make up his mind. Then he shrugged his shoulders and pushed on again, quietly, cautiously, watching each step.

As he drew closer, the loud, piercing shrieks continued. They filled his ears and echoed through the sodden marshland. It was a strange, violent sound, one that he had never heard before. He moved carefully, pushing his way through the brier thickets and around clumps of ferns that grew higher than his head. At any moment he expected some evil demon to jump out of the underbrush. His heart leaped as the screams came again. They were only a few paces away now, and they came from a thick growth of bracken ferns near the base of a lone oak tree. He moistened his lips with the tip of his tongue and clutched his spear tightly, a knot of fear in the pit of his stomach. He took a deep breath and pushed his way through the alders. Then he stepped into the clearing, ready to come face to face with the evil spirit.

Instead he saw a demon with wings, an angry eagle-owl sitting on the forest floor, protecting her nest from the little wolf dog. Even for an eagle-owl she was huge, almost as high as Tao's waist. She loomed over the wolf dog as he crept in to get beneath her wings. She flew up, snapping her beak, slashing at him with her sharp talons. She hissed and screamed, her brownish-red feathers ruffled up in bristling rage. Her glossy black pupils, ringed with orange, glared back at the wolf, daring him to try again. Once more the wolf rushed in to chase her off the nest. But the owl would not be led astray. She hovered over the three white eggs, protecting them from the hungry wolf.

For a few moments Tao stood aside, watching the battle.

He liked the eagle-owl's fierce courage. "If there be

demons," he whispered, "you must be one of them."
Yet he felt sorry for her too, for now she had a second
enemy to face. Besides, he was afraid the little wolf
dog might get hurt.

Tao lifted his spear and leaned forward to push
her away. She turned on him in savage fury, beating
him with her wings, slashing at him with her curved
talons. He threw up his arms to protect his face as
she flew at him. Again the wolf dog dashed in to
draw her off, but the feathered demon refused to be
chased away. Now the boy and wolf took turns,
taunting her, trying to divert her attention. Each
time they came too close, she turned quickly,
screaming, slashing, driving them off.

Soon Tao and the wolf dog were panting heavily as
they tried again and again to reach the eggs. But the
owl was tiring too; she was slowing down. She
rocked back and forth on her short legs, her wings
drooping, weary from the uneven fight. Now Tao
watched closely as the wolf dog attacked, each time
leading the eagle-owl farther from the nest. Then he
saw his chance. On the next rush the big owl lost her
balance, floundering on the forest floor. Before she
could recover, Tao rushed in and grabbed two of the
large white eggs. Without looking back he vaulted
away, out of danger. "Come, little friend," he
shouted to the wolf dog. "We have enough for both."
He hobbled off under the trees, the wolf dog following as the owl vented its anger in wild shrieks of
rage.

When they were far enough away, Tao stopped. Panting, he sat down with his back against the trunk of an old birch tree. He cracked one of the eggs on a stone, opened it and dipped his tongue into the thick fluid. It tasted fresh and clean. "It is good," he said. "The eggs were newly laid." Then he gave it to the wolf dog. He made a hole in the second one, tilted back his head and sucked out the contents.

The wolf dog finished his and looked up as if expecting more.

"No," said Tao. "We will let the she-owl keep her single egg. The season is early. She will lay more." He looked down at the little animal. "You are learning to hunt on your own. That is good. But it is not good to fight the eagle-owls. You must find something smaller."

The wolf tilted its head and looked up for a moment. Then, as if he understood, he ran on ahead and disappeared into the woods.

There were sandy glades within the Slough where scattered clumps of bunchgrass and bilberry bushes grew. Tao hobbled from one to another, poking with his spear, hoping to scare up hidden game. He walked slowly from bush to bush, working his way up one side of the long glade and down the other.

The morning was almost over and he was about to give up, when a swamp hare jumped out of one of the bushes and dashed across his path. Tao barely had time to brace himself. Taking quick aim, he threw his spear at the dodging animal. The weapon missed its mark and Tao groaned as the rabbit escaped.

A moment later Tao saw the wolf dog come into the glade and begin sniffing from bush to bush. The scent of the rabbit was strong, and he soon found what he was looking for. The little animal began a slow stalking movement, creeping forward on his belly. He lifted each paw slowly, setting it down in the grass carefully. Tao watched, patiently, at his end of the glade.

Once again the hare suddenly dashed out of cover. The wolf dog bounded after it, following a zigzag course, twisting and swerving with each turn of its quarry. Tao raised his spear, steadying himself as the wolf drove the rabbit directly toward him. He aimed carefully and, as the frightened animal passed, he struck it cleanly on the first throw.

As he picked up the rabbit, Tao smiled. "You will be a good hunter," he told the wolf dog. "First you find the eggs of the owl, now you find a rabbit."

Even as Tao spoke, the little wolf was running on ahead, going from bush to bush. With its head down it sniffed the ground to pick up a scent. It worked in and around the thickets and between the tussocks of grass.

Before long another rabbit leaped from under a bush. It ran around in circles, a brown whirl of fur, with the little wolf dog close on its heels. In its panic it turned and headed straight for Tao. At the last moment, it saw the boy and doubled back. Tao groaned.

The animal had escaped again. Then he felt a quick wave of relief as he saw it run directly into the waiting jaws of the wolf dog.

Tao's heart was full of joy. The sun was still high in the heavens and they already had two rabbits. He sat on his heel in the middle of the glade and with his flint knife he skinned one of the hares and fed it to the little wolf. The other rabbit he tucked under his belt to take back to camp.

As soon as the wolf dog had finished his meal, Tao put out his hand. This time the little animal allowed itself to be touched. "You are a good friend," said Tao, patting the wolf dog's head and scratching him behind the ears. "I will call you Ram, after the spirit of the hunt."

They stayed together for most of the day, roaming back and forth through the Slough, and by late afternoon Tao had three more rabbits and a leather pouch full of lemmings.

When he was ready to leave, he looked down at Ram. He wished he could take the wolf dog back to camp with him, but he knew that Volt and the other hunters would kill it. "Stay," he told Ram. "This is a good place, and here you will be safe. There is much food and you will not go hungry."

As Tao walked away, the wolf dog started to follow. The boy turned. "No, Ram," he said. "You cannot come with me. Stay here in the Slough and wait. I will come back again and we will hunt together."

The little wolf dog tilted his head to one side and Tao knew he still did not understand. "Go back," he ordered.

When Ram did not move, Tao picked up stones and handfuls of sod and threw them at the animal. "Go back," he repeated. "You cannot come with me!"

For another moment Ram stood motionless, his yellow eyes staring at Tao. But when he saw the boy reach down to pick up more stones, he turned and ran off into the Slough.

As soon as the wolf dog had disappeared, Tao hurried on his way. It was growing dark. He heard a nightjar trill. A squirrel scurried across his path and out on the plains. The prowling hyenas started their high-pitched giggles.

Even in the darkness Tao knew his way by the gray shadows of the trees, the boulders and the shape of the cliffs.

When he limped into camp, the clan women were cooking over the fires. They smiled when they saw the rabbits and the lemmings hanging from his belt. He went first to the hut of Kala and gave her a handful of mussels and three lemmings. Then he went to the center of the camp, where Volt and Garth were standing by the big fire.

The gruff leader snatched the rabbits from the boy's hand. He held them up to the light of the fire, his dark eyes wide with surprise. "These are freshly killed," he said.

Tao winced and stared at the ground. "I could not find the other," he said.

"It is good for you that you caught these," said Volt, glaring down at him. "From now on when you go out with the hunters, you will watch and learn and keep your mind on the hunting."

Tao leaned on his spear, shifting from one foot to the other. He did not want to disobey. Yet the anger within him would not let him be silent. I have Ram now, he thought. With the wolf dog I can bring back more food than the hunters. Instead he said, "I will hunt alone. What I catch I will bring back to the camp."

Volt shook his head violently, the ring of bear claws around his neck rattling. "You are like a stone!" he roared. "You learn nothing. I try to tell you, but you do not listen." The big man threw up his hands and looked hopelessly over his shoulder at Garth, who had come up behind him. "Go then," he said to Tao. "Go your own way. But hear my words, you will eat only when you bring in food."

Once again Tao felt the heat of anger rising in his cheeks. "Maybe if we had a wolf dog," he said, "it would help with the hunting."

Volt's face grew red with rage, the livid scars standing out on his cheek. "We will have no evil wolf dogs at this camp!" he shouted. "They are a curse of demons. We will hunt like men, not like evil spirits."

"If wolf dogs are evil, then why do the Mountain People hunt with them?" asked Tao, surprised that he was speaking to Volt this way.

Startled by the boy's impudence, Volt spat on the ground and grunted. "Enough!" he shouted. "If you would hunt with an evil wolf dog, then go, go live with the Mountain People."

Garth threw back his head and laughed grimly. "Cross the river into their land and they will track you down like a jackal."

Tao shrugged. He felt there was little use in talking to these men, who would listen only to demons and evil spirits.

Later that night Tao sat by the fire in front of Kala's hut. He looked up at the overhanging cliffs and saw the Endless Flame burning bright in front of the entrance to Big Cave. He had spent many winters in the protection of its shelter. But deep inside, through twisting tunnels and narrow passageways, lay the Secret Cavern. Only the Chosen Ones had ever seen it, but Tao had heard about it many times. It was a huge chamber, its walls covered with life-size paintings of horses, bison and lions. Even the ceilings were painted with pictures of deer, bear and boars. Here the rituals of manhood were held, here the Chosen Ones were selected.

Tao knew that each clan had its own secret place, a special chamber hidden far back in the cliffs. Each clan had its image makers also, two or three Chosen Ones picked by the elders to paint in the caves.

But Graybeard was the old master, the shaman, wandering from clan to clan teaching and painting images of the great game animals to bring good luck in the hunting.

Tao thought of this often. If only he were born of a leader, or even a hunter, then he might someday become a Chosen One. Many times he had asked Kala about his parents. But each time she shook her head. "You are too young," she always said. "Besides, it does not matter."

But now he was older and it did matter.

▪ FOUR

Kala was alone with the new child as Tao stooped into the hut. Inside was a bed of straw and a smaller one for the child. A small cookfire burned near the back of the hut, sending a thin trail of blue smoke up through the vent hole. Kala's gray hair hung down over her shoulders, and her face was lined from many hard winters. She often told Tao she had a wrinkle for every fall of snow. In spite of years of carrying firewood, skinning deer, making robes and sewing clothing, Kala could still smile. She smiled with good strong teeth, strong from chewing on pelts and skins to make them soft. Always Kala spoke the truth, which often angered the elders, but they let her alone because she was wise and knew much history of the clan.

Before Tao spoke she laid the new baby on an antelope robe, then stepped out of the hut, pretending to look around. When she came back she squatted down crosslegged in front of the boy. She picked up one of the black mussels Tao had given her. "You have been down in the Slough," she said.

Tao was startled. He was surprised that she had guessed.

"It is the only place near where these can be found," she said, clicking her tongue.

Tao saw the smile behind her frown. "You know the Slough?" he whispered, as if sharing a secret between them.

"I used to go there when I was a girl. It was a good place, filled with many berries, many mushrooms and fish." She smiled as she remembered. "But that was before the bad thing happened, before it became a place of evil."

"What bad thing, Kala?"

The old woman shook her head. "It was a long time ago."

"It is wrong," said Tao, "that the clan people should go hungry when there is food nearby."

Kala threw up her hands. "You wish to question the elders?"

"No," said Tao. "It would do no good."

Tao looked at this old woman whose eyes were still young and green like the willow leaves. She was wise and good and he could not have asked for a better mother. Yet he knew she was not of his blood. After a long silence he said, "Kala, I am fourteen summers now and I wish to know about my mother and father."

"You will not give up," she said. "Perhaps it is better that you do not know."

"But I must find out," said Tao, "if I am ever to enter the ritual of manhood. In the eyes of the elders it is very important. If I am the son of a leader or a hunter, like Garth, I might someday become a Chosen One. Then I can draw and paint."

Kala shook her head sadly. "You dream, boy. But your dreams are not true. As long as there are taboos, it can never be."

"But how can it hurt to know about my father?"

Kala placed the mussel shell into a bowl made from an empty ox bone. "Of that I will not tell you. I am one of the few who know and it is a thing we do not speak of."

"Is it such a terrible thing?"

"Yes," said the old woman. "It is a terrible thing."

Tao was silent for a moment. She will not say it, he thought, but it is because I have a bad foot. I do not walk as the others. That too is why I can never be a Chosen One. Tao sighed. He knew it would do no good to press her for an answer. "My mother, then," he said. "Tell me about my mother."

The old woman nodded. She settled back on her bearskin rug, the strings of gray hair hanging down over her face. There was a peaceful look in her eyes as she spoke. "Your mother was Vedra of the Mountain People. She was sixteen summers, and she was captured in one of the raids during a summer famine. You were early-born in the middle of a cold winter like the one that has just passed."

Tao's heart was pounding. He had never heard his mother's name before. "Vedra." He repeated the name quietly—"Vedra"—his dark eyes shining in the dim light, the soft sound rolling off the end of his tongue. "Vedra of the Mountain People."

"It is the law of the clan," the old woman continued, "that weak and crippled children be taken up among the boulders and left for the hyenas. But your mother would not let you go. She sat in a corner of Big Cave, holding you to her breast, keeping you warm, rocking back and forth, singing. Again and again they tried to take you away, but she fought like a cave lion, screaming, biting, refusing to give you up.

"All through the long snows she kept you alive. I brought her food. She would not leave the cave, and it was a winter where the winds found their way into the mountain. Before the moons of summer she grew weak. When she died your father ordered that you be left to die among the boulders. I brought you back and raised you for my own. The elders shook their heads, but I did not care. The man who is your father called it an evil curse."

"That is why you will not tell me his name?"

"That is why I will never tell you his name."

"Then tell me more about my mother," said Tao. "What was she like?"

"She was only a girl," said Kala, "but she had the sense and wisdom of a woman. Always she worked with her hands. She made many things from the earth and waters. From pebbles and the bones of fish she made necklaces; from ivory and antlers she made beads and bracelets and needles; even from the grass of the fields she made headbands and rings for the hair. Everyone loved the things she made, and she gave them away freely."

Tao looked up, his dark eyes wide as he smiled. "Then she too was a maker? She too saw pictures in the sky and the meadows?"

"Yes," said the old woman. "I am sure she gave you the eyes to see beauty in the things around you, the animals, the trees, the mountains. I saw this even when you were a small child. You reached out for the flowers in the fields and you loved to watch birds and squirrels flying through the oak trees. It is the thing that makes you different from others. It is the thing they do not always understand."

Tao's thoughts were racing ahead, his mind filled with new ideas. "I am happy now," he said. A shadow flickered across his face. "Now I know what I must do. If I cannot be a Chosen One, I will live away from the clan. I will find a cave high up in the cliffs, above the boulders. I will live out on the grasslands and in the oak forest." He hesitated, his voice falling. "And I will hunt in the Slough where the fruit and game are plentiful. I will be a man in my own way."

"You are a dreamer," Kala smiled.

Tao shook his head. "No, Kala, look at me. My arms are strong. For three summers I have hunted and brought back food for Kala."

She looked at him darkly. "Hunt then," she said,

"but do not make an enemy of the clan. If you make images or go into forbidden places, be sure you are not seen. Go your own way if you wish, but be careful."

Tao reached out and touched her gently on the arm. "Thank you, Kala," he said. "Thank you for many things, but especially for what you have told me. I will come back often and bring you food."

Tao went out and crouched by the big fire in the center of the camp. He was thinking about what Kala had said when he heard a soft whimpering sound coming from beyond the light of the fire. He jumped up and saw a pair of yellow eyes staring at him from out of the darkness. Tao gasped in surprise. It was Ram. The foolish wolf dog had followed him.

■ FIVE

Throughout the little camp the hunters heard the whimpering sound too.

"A wolf, a wolf!" shouted one.

They reached for their spears, grabbed flaming torches from the fire, and rushed out into the darkness to search the bushes and scrubwood.

Volt heard the noise. Throwing his deerskin robe across his shoulders, he strode into the firelight. "What is it?"

"Wolf!" a hunter repeated.

"Kill the evil beast," shouted Volt, "or it will be a curse on our camp." He followed the hunters, shaking his spear.

Tao stood at the edge of the camp, listening to the men moving through the forest. He heard them beating the bushes with their spears and he saw their torches bobbing in the darkness. He tried to think of some way to save the little wolf. To raise his voice or call out would only bring the hunters running.

Somehow he had to find Ram before they did. He grabbed a flaming stick from the fire and limped out into the night. He heard the hunters crashing through the underbrush and he knew they were forming a wide circle, getting ready to close in and surround the wolf dog.

Tao held his torch high, trying to see through the dark branches of the buckthorn trees. "Ram," he whispered, his eyes searching the dim light. "Where are you, Ram?"

Moments passed. The little animal had been frightened off by the noise. But Tao was sure he must be near. He called again, softly: "Ram."

Nothing moved. His torch flickered and the waving shadows of the buckthorn trees played tricks on his eyes. His heart sank as he heard the hunters come closer. The ring of spears was tightening. Just then a gray shadow moved across his path, slinking out of the darkness. Tao waited as the animal crept toward him, whimpering. It was Ram. Tao leaned down and pushed him back. "Go," he whispered. "Get away, quickly."

Ram refused to move. He stood there looking up at Tao, a fearful look in his yellow eyes.

Tao picked up a stick as if to throw. "Go," he ordered sharply.

But it was too late. Tao heard the voices of the

hunters only a few paces away. The little wolf was nearly surrounded.

Quickly Tao sprang forward. He thrust his torch into the damp earth, quenching the flame, then threw it aside. He curled the leg of his bad foot around the shaft of his spear and vaulted ahead. "Wolf, wolf!" he shouted loud enough for the hunters to hear. "Come," he whispered fiercely to the wolf dog.

Stumbling, lurching through the forest, Tao heard their pounding feet as the hunters picked up the trail. Without looking back, Tao hurdled over the ground, dodging between the trees and bushes. The wolf dog followed close behind as Tao ran into the night. Branches whipped across his face, tree roots caught at his feet, holding him back. But if he could run fast enough, long enough, he knew he would outrun the hunters and save Ram.

Breathing hard, he pushed his way through the underbrush, listening to the grunts and shouts of the angry men as they came after him. He ran faster and faster, twisting and turning through the trees and brush, trying to throw them off the track.

But they kept up the pace, crashing through the forest not far behind him.

He stumbled on blindly through the blackness, vaulting along on the shaft of his spear. His arms grew heavy, his legs were like stones. The trees, the shadows, the night itself became a tangled wall, holding him back as he plunged into the darkness.

How long he ran Tao did not know, but little by little the shouts and footsteps began to fade. He continued on until he was sure it was safe. Panting and out of breath, he had almost reached the river. He stopped and looked around. The wolf dog was not behind him. "Ram," he whispered, searching the darkness. "Where are you?"

He waited, listening. Nothing moved. He wondered if Ram had been caught. Maybe the wolf dog had been killed and the hunters had turned back. But he had heard nothing. Silence and darkness added to his gloom. His head throbbed and he turned to go back. Then once again he saw Ram slink out of the shadows, whimpering, creeping up to him on his belly.

With a wave of relief Tao stooped down and threw his arms around the animal's shoulder. He spoke to him firmly. "You cannot come into the camp of the clan people," he said. "They have no love for the wolves. They will kill you." Tao pushed the little animal away. "Go," he said, sharply. "Go back and wait in the Slough."

Ram looked up, panting, his tongue lolling out of the side of his mouth.

Tao reached down to pick up a stone. Immediately the wolf dog turned. He looked back once or twice, then disappeared into the darkness. Tao grinned. At last he had found a way to make the wolf dog understand.

Tao walked lightly as he returned to camp, but he put on an angry face. "I could not catch him," he said to the hunters who had gathered by the fire. "But he is far gone. He will not return."

Volt grunted, slamming his fist into the palm of his hand. "It is an evil sign," he said, rubbing his scarred cheek with the back of his hand, his dark shaggy head nodding. "It is an evil sign."

"We must watch for him and kill him," said Garth. Sometimes Garth sounded more like Volt than Volt himself. "We will not let him get away again." Tao felt his stomach turn.

The next morning, after he had banked the fires with three other younger boys of the clan, Tao walked out along the foot of the limestone cliffs, far away from camp. The ash-gray walls loomed high over his head and he came to a spot with many caves. This is a good place, he thought. Here I can make images away from the eyes of Volt and the hunters. Yet it is close enough to visit Kala and bring back food to her and the clan people.

He looked up at the steep rocky ledges and started to climb. It was not easy, but he was able to cling to the crevices and stunted pine shrubs growing out of the cliff wall.

The first two caves he saw were not to his liking. One was too small and the walls were rough and uneven. The second had an animal smell. Tao did not wish to share his home with a leopard or a bear. About halfway up he found a third one. It looked out over the flat valley. He saw no pugmarks and he was sure it was deserted. It was about ten spear lengths long and opened into a small cavern. The walls were smooth with only a few breaks or cracks.

This is what I am looking for, he thought. This will be a good place to stay.

Certain that he had found what he wanted, Tao spent four days filling his cave with dried grass, firewood and kindling. Kala gave him a bearskin robe and a tallow lamp made from a large cockleshell filled with animal fat and a wick made of peat moss. She showed him how to dry cattail roots and bur-reed tubers for cooking. She wrapped live embers in a handful of wet grass, placed them in a hollow bone and gave them to him for his fire.

When his cave was ready, Tao went down to the little stream that ran through the willow wood and found a bank of yellow clay. He scooped out some of the clammy substance, rolled it into long pieces and let them dry in the sun. He picked oak twigs and burned them in the fire to make sticks of charcoal.

This done, he stepped back and looked around his little cave. With his chunks of clay and charcoal and a handful of moss for a wiper, he was ready to become a maker of images. He had no picture or sketch to work from. He would have to draw from memory.

He picked up a stick of dried clay. It felt good in

his hand and he made a mark on the gray wall. It showed up bold and sharp.

I will draw a horse, he thought. Even though no one else will see it, I will know what I have done and I will feel good.

He started with the head, drawing the long face and the square jaw. Next he sketched in the ears and the gentle curve of the neck. He worked quickly, trying to see in his mind's eye how the horses looked when he saw them out in the valley. With firm strokes of the chalk he drew in the muscular body, the shoulder, the arched rump and the tail.

Then he tried to draw the legs. His hand hesitated. Did the front leg bend just below the body, or farther down? He could not remember. The hind legs were even more difficult. He thought they slanted toward the tail, then bent forward at the knee. But where was the knee? He wasn't sure. He went on, his hand moving across the wall. When he was finished he stepped back. It's not right, he thought. The legs are all wrong.

Impatiently he rubbed it out with a handful of moss and started again. This time he drew the body first, adding the legs and the long, sweeping tail. But when he drew the head, it was too big for the body. He shook his head peevishly. "It's no good," he said. "It looks more like a bear."

He tried again and again, but each time it only seemed to get worse. He tried drawing a row of heads, then a row of bodies, but they didn't match. He shook his head in frustration and threw the chalk against the wall, where it broke in a hundred pieces. "I'll never learn," he said.

He sat on the cold floor, brooding for a while. Then he picked up another piece of chalk and tried again. All day long he drew horses—small horses, running horses, all kinds of horses. He forgot to eat the ground plums Kala had given him, he forgot to make his drink of birch tea. The harder he tried, the more trouble he had. He dropped his chalk and lay down on his bearskin rug, tired, angry, and discouraged, and he fell asleep.

When he awoke the next morning it was quiet. He looked around. There was no smell of Kala's fire, no sound of voices. Then he remembered he was alone, and he was hungry. He climbed down the cliff and made his way across the valley. When he reached the river he turned west and continued on until he came to the Slough.

The trees and vines were green with new leaves. The black loam was thick with uncoiling ferns, and the dank bottomland smelled sweet and earthy. He stopped for a moment and looked around to be sure no one had seen him, then he pushed on through the thickets and into the Slough. He had long forgotten about evil spirits and demons, and he stopped at the stream to feast on watercress and mussels. No longer hungry, he went down into the glades, where he hoped to catch a rabbit or even a young pig.

He was searching around the clumps of dwarf oaks when he saw Ram come running through the tall grass. Tao smiled broadly. He was surprised to see how well the little wolf looked. Ram had gained weight and his silver-gray fur coat was clean and smooth.

The animal crept up to him, whimpering, holding its head low. As Tao reached down to pet it, it rolled over on its back and licked his hand. "You are growing," said Tao. "Someday you will be a fine wolf dog. But you must learn to stay away from the clan people and the hunters. Come," he said. "Now we will hunt together."

All that morning they hunted through the Slough, catching rabbits, field mice and a willow grouse. With Ram trotting by his side, Tao started back for his little cave. He looked around again as he crossed the open valley to be sure no one was watching. Once in the shelter of the cave, they were safe. Here Tao started his fire from the old embers and roasted their grouse and rabbits. The sun had not yet set behind the hills, and golden shafts of light streamed in through the cave entrance. Ram was standing in the opening, and, as Tao ate, he saw the wolf dog's body outlined against the pink sky-line.

Quickly he pushed aside his food and picked up a piece of chalk. He began sketching hurriedly, trying to catch the animal's form and shape. He worked swiftly, his hand gliding over the cave wall. He drew in the sharp muzzle, the pointed ears, erect and alert. His hand flew in curves and swoops, catching the lithe beauty of the silver-gray body.

He stepped back and looked at the picture. Then he picked up a stick of charcoal and added the slitted eyes and the coal-black nose. This time he was pleased and he did not rub out the drawing. He knew now that if he had something to go by, something to guide his eye, he could make an image true and without mistakes.

■ SIX

Later that spring, Tao and Ram roamed the valley and woodlands. Mostly they hunted in the Slough, where the game was plentiful and where they were not likely to be seen by Volt and the other hunters.

Far to the north, in the high mountains, the retreating glaciers sent down torrents of cold water to form crystal-clear lakes, rippling streams and endless swamplands. In the icy creeks Tao and Ram caught trout and pike. Sometimes, in the distance, they saw the big brown bears fishing along the edges of the sandbars, slapping salmon out of the water with their great paws.

When the hunting was good and they caught much game, Tao left Ram in the little cave and returned to camp with rabbits, quail, geese and strings of salmon for Kala and the clan people.

One afternoon Volt and Garth were standing in the

clearing as the boy came in. Volt scratched his head with a big hairy hand, squinting. "You bring in much game," he said. "Yet you say you hunt alone."

Tao did not want to lie. Yet he knew, if he told the truth, that everything he had would be taken from him—the cave, the paintings, the wolf dog, everything. He stared hard at the ground. "I hunt with no man," he said.

"Then you have found a place of plenty," said Garth curiously. "If that is so, you will tell us where it is."

Once again Tao hesitated. He dare not talk of the Slough, but he could tell about the other places. "If you will go one day's walk to the spruce forests where the creeks run down to the big waters, there the hunters will find salmon. But the brown bears are taking many. The hunters will have to hurry."

Volt grunted, shook his head and walked away with Garth behind him. Tao knew it was not easy for the big leader to ask a boy where game was to be found. Yet the small band of clan hunters could not cover all the land.

Whenever Tao saw the hunters in his area, he stayed in his little cave. Here, with Ram lying at his feet, he practiced his drawing, covering the walls with pictures of bears, bison and mammoths. He was never satisfied with these. But when he made pictures of Ram, he felt his images were good.

Down near the glades a big glacier lake extended a long blue finger into the Slough. It was a place of

beauty, a place where Tao could always find something new and surprising, and it soon became one of
his favorite haunts. Here he saw the tall white
cranes stalking through the reeds, jabbing for minnows and crayfish. He watched the screaming fish-
eagles swoop down to snatch squirming eels and
perch out of the glistening waters.

One day, as the lake lay steaming in the early
morning sun, he and Ram walked around the
marshy shoreline, hunting for duck eggs. They had
just come through a stand of reed grass when Tao
saw an animal, the size of a large horse, feeding in
the shallows. The boy drew in his breath. It was a
giant deer. He had heard about such creatures, but
they were rare and only a few hunters had ever seen
one.

Unaware of danger, the deer stood in the knee-
deep water, raking up strings of water lilies. Its huge
rack of antlers spread out from its head like two
great hands with the palms up and the sharp prongs
or fingers curving inward.

Tao watched as the deer came closer. He kept his
hand on Ram's shoulder to hold him back. The wolf
was eager to begin the chase, and Tao could feel the
tension in its body. "No, Ram," he whispered. "You
are no match for the great deer. In the water you
would have no chance."

Tao knew the big deer could not outrun the wolf,
but with its massive spread of antlers it could be
dangerous.

Boy and wolf stood on the edge of the lake, watching quietly. They were so taken up with the sight of the huge animal that they failed to hear the footsteps of the stranger as he came up behind them.

It was an old man, thin and gaunt, with squint creases at the corners of his deep-blue eyes. His face was covered with a long, almost white beard and he carried a long wooden spear and a deerskin bag slung over his left shoulder.

He stopped a short distance away and watched them for a while. Then, as if not to startle them, he coughed lightly.

Ram spun around, snarling, the hair along the back of his neck bristling with anger.

The big deer stopped feeding. It threw up its head and splashed away across the shallows.

Still standing at the water's edge, Tao turned to face the hunter. His heart was pounding. He had broken many taboos—he walked on forbidden land, he made images on cave walls and he hunted with a wolf dog. Now this stranger would be a witness.

Tao placed his hand on Ram's shoulder and ordered him to stay. Then he limped slowly toward the man, trying to act unafraid.

The old man looked down at him from under bushy eyebrows. There was no anger in his face, only a touch of mild surprise. He saw the bad foot and the air of boyish defiance. "You are Tao of the Valley People," he said.

"You know my name?" asked Tao, startled.

"Yes," said the old man. "I travel far to paint images in the secret caverns, and I hear much."

Tao gasped. He felt a mixture of dismay and awe. The stranger standing before him was Graybeard, the Cave Painter, the shaman of all the clans. Never did he think he would meet such a great one.

"I also know you hunt on forbidden land," said Graybeard.

The boy winced and shifted from one foot to the other. "It is forbidden only because of the demons and evil spirits," he said, his voice cracking.

"And you are not afraid of demons?"

"I have heard the wailing screams and the wild howls, but they are the cries of the eagle-owl and the loons. If there are other demons I have never seen one."

The old man leaned on his spear. "You also hunt with a wolf dog. That too is taboo in your clan."

For a moment Tao was quiet. Then he swallowed hard and said, "The people of my clan are starving. The Slough is full of game. With the wolf dog I bring them much food."

Graybeard nodded. "You are not afraid of demons, you do not believe in evil spirits and, for you, taboos melt away like the winter snows."

"I am sorry," said Tao, "but I do not believe these things are bad. The animals, the birds, the trees give us food and clothing. Yet our leaders see only evil."

Graybeard nodded. Tao was sure he saw a glint of understanding in the old man's eye.

"And you know better than the leaders?" said Graybeard.

"No," said Tao. "I only know that the Slough is a place of many good things. Here I find food. I watch the animals and birds . . . I feel good here."

Graybeard looked out across the blue lake. "And now you watch the great antlered one?"

"Yes," said Tao. "I have never seen a giant deer before."

"There are many far to the north, near the ice country," said Graybeard. "They come down this way sometimes when the snows are bad."

Ram was standing behind Tao, a half snarl still curled on his lips.

The old man looked at the wolf, unafraid. "How long have you hunted with the wolf dog?"

Tao stopped to think. "Since the end of the snows."

"And by what name do you call him?"

"I call him Ram."

The old man smiled.

"You think it is good to have a wolf dog?" asked Tao.

"Yes," said Graybeard. "They help much with the hunting and they protect the camp at night."

"Our leader, Volt, hates the wolf dogs," said Tao. "He believes they are a curse of evil and he will have none of them."

"I know your leader well," said Graybeard. "He is a good man, but too often he dreams of spirits and demons."

Tao came a step closer, whispering. "I have told no one about Ram."

"I will say nothing," said Graybeard. "I come only to paint in the Secret Cavern."

Tao felt a wave of relief. He knew Graybeard would keep his word.

"The herds are coming back," said the old man, nodding. "They will be here when the fields are green with new grass. I have come from the other camps with the news. Now I will paint images of the great beasts in the secret caverns to bring good hunting."

Tao wished to hear more about the image making and the painting, but he saw that the old man was tired. "Will you come and share food with us?" asked Tao. "We have a small cave on the other side of the valley."

Graybeard leaned against the trunk of a birch tree. His spear rested on the crook of his arm as he rubbed his eyes with the back of his hands. "Yes," he said, "it will be good to rest."

■ SEVEN

They walked slowly, making their way up through the uncoiling ferns and budding buckthorn trees. On the way Tao had many questions.

"Other clans have kept wolf dogs," he said. "Why does Volt hate them so much?"

The old man stopped to catch his breath, coughing slightly. "You have seen Volt's face?" he asked. "You have seen the scars and the look of meanness?"

Tao frowned. "This was done by a wolf dog?"

"Volt thinks so," said Graybeard. "He was only a child, but his father said it was so."

"I do not think a wolf dog would do that," said Tao.

"Nor do I," said the old man. "There were many hyenas at the time. But his father believed in demons and he said it was the curse of a wolf. Volt will not say otherwise. That is why this place is forbidden."

"You mean it happened in the Slough?"

"Yes," said Graybeard. "Volt was here with his mother, gathering berries. Some beast attacked them. Volt was badly clawed. His mother was killed. So this became a place of evil. Now others hear the wild cries and wailing and think of demons."

When Tao and the old man came to the open valley, the boy looked around slowly.

"Yes," said Graybeard, "it is well to keep the wolf dog out of sight."

Tao agreed, then added, "But if Volt could see how well Ram hunts, maybe he would change his mind."

The old man shrugged. "Volt knows only the world of evil spirits. Unless there is some omen or sign, I do not think he will change his mind."

"You know much about the clan peoples," said Tao.

"For twenty summers now I have gone from clan to clan, painting in the caves, bringing news, and helping them when they are sick." He stopped for a moment, running a knotted hand through his beard. "I have seen many young boys grow up to become hunters and young women become mothers."

Tao's heart leaped. A ray of hope sparkled in his eyes. "You knew my mother, my father?"

Graybeard shook his head. "No, I only know that

your mother died shortly after you were born and that you were raised by Kala."

"Then you know Kala?"

The old man hummed softly, then said, "Yes, we grew up together. But that was many summers ago, before you were born and before I became a shaman."

"Then you are also of the Valley People?"

"Once. I left before my sixteenth summer. Now I am of all the clans."

When they reached the foot of the cliffs, they began to climb. They went slowly, for the old man stopped to rest many times.

At the entrance to the little cave, the boy stepped aside to let the old one go in first.

As soon as his eyes became adjusted to the dim light, Graybeard saw the drawings on the wall. He saw the sketches of the wolf dog, the charcoal drawings of the cave bear, the owl and the salmon. He stood there for a long time, looking from one to another. Then he saw the clay chalk and the charcoal sticks lying on the floor.

Tao waited tensely. This man was the master. His words would mean much. He bit his lip and took a deep breath as he waited for the old man to speak.

Graybeard turned slowly. "You did these?"

"Yes," said Tao, his chest swelling with pride.

The old man looked at the drawings once again, measuring them with his eye. Then he rubbed his hand over them lightly and blew the chalk from his fingers. "Who showed you how to do this?"

"No one," said Tao. "I taught myself."

The old man nodded. He studied the pictures again, running his long bony finger over the lines, following the curves of the drawings, all the while mumbling to himself. Then he stepped back. His wrinkled face changed into an angry frown. With both hands he leaned down and picked up fistfuls of dirt and soot from the cave floor. He rubbed them across the wall, smearing them over the drawings, covering them up.

Tao staggered backward in shocked surprise, disappointment and hurt showing on his face. "They are not good?" he asked.

Graybeard was breathing hard, trying to control a fit of coughing. "Young fool," he cried. "Do you not know better than to make images or signs where they might be seen?"

Tao was numb. He could no longer think. "Then they are not good?" he asked again.

The old man shook his head, his eyes flashing with displeasure. "It does not matter," he said. "Good or bad, you are not a Chosen One. They could kill you for this."

Tao's fists were clenched tight at his sides. Tears filled his eyes and he spoke in a choked voice. "I do not care," he said. "It is only that I would like to be an image maker. I have thought about it for a long time. Even when I sleep I dream of it. I wish to be a cave painter, as you are."

The old man looked down at him, anger still flashing in his eyes. "It is taboo," he said harshly. "Whether you believe in it or not makes no difference. It is taboo. It is the law of the clans and you must live by it."

■ EIGHT

The old man walked back and forth, his feet shuffling across the cave floor. He stopped at the entrance and looked out across the valley. He was still breathing heavily, but the storm within him was over. "I am sorry," he said. "It is a thing that must be handed down. My father was a cave painter. Now I am one. That is the way it has always been. It cannot start from nothing." He stopped his pacing and looked down at Tao. "You must learn to live with things you cannot change."

Tao sighed deeply, biting his lip, trying to forget.

A short while later they sat crosslegged on the cave floor, eating freshwater mussels that Tao had scooped from the creek. With sharp flint knives they pried open the blue-black shells and picked out the soft flesh within.

The smell of birch tea filled the little cave as the leather sack brewed over the open fire. They ate in silence for a while. Finally Tao spoke. "Then it can never be?"

The old man nodded impatiently. "I tell you again, unless you are born of a leader or chosen by the elders it would not be accepted." He opened another shell and ate the contents, washing it down with a sip of birch tea. "For a thousand summers it has been in the minds of the people and cannot be changed."

"And I must not do this thing I love. I must not make images?"

Graybeard looked out through the cave entrance, gazing off into the distance. He tugged at his beard for a moment, deep in thought. "Yes, yes, do it if you wish. But do not let the others know. They would not understand. And always rub out your images when you are finished."

The old man glanced at the cave wall where he had blotted out the pictures. "You have made a good beginning," he said, "but you have much to learn about form and shape. You must study the animals closely. See how they look when they run or lie down. Notice the color of their fur in the bright sun or under the shadow of a tree."

Graybeard smiled. He had completely forgotten his outburst and his eyes shone as he spoke. "Go up on the high plains and watch Saxon, the sacred bull. See how the heavy muscles ripple beneath his shoulders. Watch how he moves his head and remember the angry fire in his eyes. Then put it all into your image."

"It is something like magic," said Tao, his voice rising with excitement.

The old man picked up his deerskin bag, shaking it, rattling the contents within. "Here is the real magic," he said. "With these graven stones I can speak to the spirits of the animals and bring good hunting."

He took out seven flat stones, each larger than his open hand, each engraved with the figure of a different animal. He picked out one and held it up for Tao to see. On it was the engraving of a mammoth.

Tao gasped. "It is the mountain-that-walks."

"Yes," said Graybeard. "Three summers past they came through the valley and I drew this sketch."

"They have not been here since."

"That is true," said the old man, "but now, from this sketch, I can draw others on the walls of the Secret Cavern. I can draw line for line, making the shape exactly as it was when I first saw it. In this way I can speak to the spirits of the great beasts and call them back to the valley."

With the point of his flint knife Graybeard began copying the picture on the dirt floor of the cave. "Here," he said. "First make a large outline of the whole animal. Next find the high point of the shoulder. Then slope the back all the way down to the tail." Graybeard swung his hand over the drawing, his eyes shining again as he drew the legs, the feet and the trunk, using short strokes to show the hair and fur.

Tao leaned forward, watching closely.

Slowly the rough picture of a mammoth began to take shape as the old man sketched in the curved tusks and the small beady eye. "You must do this over and over," said Graybeard. "That is the way you learn. But I must warn you again, rub out your image as soon as you are finished."

Graybeard stood up and erased the drawing with the toe of his deerskin sandal. "Now I must go to the camp of your people," he said. "Tonight there will be the celebration, and the ritual of the hunt."

Since he was not a Chosen One, Tao could not go, and he was sorry to see Graybeard leave. There was so much more he wanted to know. He got up, not looking directly at the old man. "I will go with you part of the way," he said.

They climbed down the ledge, with the sun shining in their eyes, and started out along the foot of the cliffs. Tao hopped along, now using his spear as a crutch with Ram trotting at his heels.

"You will have to go more slowly if I am to keep up," said Graybeard, stifling a cough.

Tao slowed his pace to that of the old man's. "If I went to the Mountain People," he said, "maybe they would accept me as a cave painter."

The old man stopped. He shook his head. "You do not understand," he said. "The Mountain People, the Lake People, the Valley People, they are all the same. Their life is filled with magic, taboos and evil spirits. If you cross the river into their land, you will not be welcome."

"Yet you travel from clan to clan without harm," said Tao.

"I have told you, I was born into the spirit world through my father. Now I can go where I please and do magic. By striking stones together I can make fire. By rubbing a dab of mud on a skin hut I can make a barren woman bring forth a child. By drawing the outline of a beast on a cave wall I can bring good hunting."

They walked on in silence again, with Tao deep in thought. Then he said, "Even though you can do all these things, are you saying it is not true, it is not really magic?"

Graybeard shrugged and tugged at his beard. "I do not know," he said. "Perhaps it is nothing more than words. Perhaps it is nothing more than shadows. Yet I am sure it brings hope to the people and boldness to the hunters. Many times the things I foretell do not happen. The people never question it. If the thing I foretell comes to pass, they are happy. One thing I know: if they wish to call it magic, then let it be so. If I try to tell them otherwise, they will be angry."

"Here," said Graybeard, stopping once again. "I will show you something they call magic." He reached into his deerskin pouch and took out a flat, round object. He held it in the palm of his hand and it glistened in the sunlight like silver fire. "This is a shining stone," he said. "It was dug out of the earth and polished in the sand by my father many summers ago."

They were standing in the open with the blazing sun high in the west. Graybeard walked slowly around the boy, flashing the sunlight off the glittering stone. Suddenly he pointed it directly at Tao's face. The boy threw up his hands, his eyes blinded by the light.

Graybeard smiled and placed the shining stone back into the deerskin pouch. "You see, it is not magic. It is only the power of the sun, nothing more. A long time ago it saved me from an angry bear."

When they reached the edge of the oak forest, Tao slowed his steps. "It is best if I stop here," he said. "I cannot take Ram into camp and it would be dangerous to go too close."

The old man agreed. He hummed softly and began to make ready his magic. He opened his leather pouch and brought out an ivory amulet and a necklace of bear's teeth and put them around his neck. From under his robe he took out a bison horn. He raised it to his lips and blew a long, trumpeting blast that echoed through the forest. The effort produced a spasm of coughs. "I can no longer blow as long or as loud as I used to," he said. Then he looked down at Tao and smiled, a sly twinkle in his deep-blue eyes. "Now I am ready."

Tao watched the old man disappear into the oak forest. He heard the trumpet blare again and again. He knew the women and children would go into hiding and the camp would become deathly still.

As Graybeard entered the clearing, the hunters would gather around, waiting for him to speak, eager for word of the coming hunt and news of the other clans. Then, as it became dark, the rituals would begin.

Tao and Ram returned to the little cave, where the boy placed some kindling in the circle of stones that was his hearth. He blew on the live embers from the old fire and soon had the flames dancing again. He fed Ram, then, squatting on his heels, he brewed up some birch tea and roasted pieces of squirrel meat on a stick. When he was finished, he stretched out on his bearskin robe and stared into the fire.

He remembered five summers past, when he was still a child. He was peering through the opening of Kala's skin hut when he first saw Graybeard in the light of the big fire, speaking to the hunters.

"Hunters of the Valley People!" Graybeard had shouted. "The great beasts are coming back. The spotted horses and the tarpans will soon be here. The bison will cross the high plains; the red deer will gather in the spruce wood." His voice was clear and loud then. "We must be brave and strong. We must run as fast as the deer and throw our spears straight, then will there be much meat and skins to cover our bodies and warm our women and children in the winter. Let us go now, into the Secret Cavern, and make images to please the spirits of the great beasts."

The men listened and became restless and eager to go. Some of them stood up, chanting and singing. Others began to dance, their ivory amulets and bone bracelets jingling and flashing in the firelight. One played a simple flute made of a hollow bone with a hole drilled on top. He shuffled around the fire, playing the same two notes over and over as the hunters continued their dance.

Tao had seen Graybeard climb up the path to the entrance of the Big Cave, followed by the hunters, carrying spears and torches. Then he could see them no more. But he knew they went far back through the winding, twisting tunnels of the cliffs and into the Secret Cavern. There, together with a few of the Chosen Ones, Graybeard painted images of the great beasts and asked the blessing of the spirits of the hunt.

Tao remembered what happened the next day, too. The hunters went out into the spruce forest and up onto the high plains and across the valley to meet the great beasts. They were gone for four days. They brought back much food, and skins from which to make clothing, and bones and horns to make tools and ornaments. Some of the young men came back as brave hunters, some came back with terrible wounds, and two did not come back at all. The day after that there was another ceremony. This time it was sad and there was much crying and wailing.

NINE

The days were growing warmer as the sun climbed high into the heavens. The open valley was a sea of waving grass, with scattered clumps of birch and willow trees, thick with new green and yellow leaves.

Slowly some of the great game herds came back grazing and browsing across the land. Antelope and deer came first, wandering in small family groups followed by bands of horses, the mares and colts grazing under the watchful eyes of stallions. The roving herds of animals increased and filled the land.

The hunting was good now, and the clan had plenty to eat. There were many new hides, too, and the women sat around the fires beneath the cliffs sewing boots, leggings and robes to replace the worn-out clothing of the year before.

As Graybeard suggested, Tao began studying the

animals more closely. He watched the loons and the great white swans feeding on the lake in the early morning mists. Twice he saw a cave lion stalking across the valley, its tawny coat blending with the buff meadowgrass. Together with Ram, he climbed the rocky passes to see the horned ibex and the mountain rams standing sentinel on the snowy peaks.

Then, one morning, he took Ram up to the top of the cliffs. There they looked out over a sweeping plateau of high plains. It stretched beyond the horizon, and not far away Tao saw Saxon, the sacred bull. Heavy bodied, thick shouldered and sturdy, Saxon looked like a huge black monster standing in the middle of the plains.

His eyesight was poor, but his sense of smell was keen, and he soon picked up the man scent as it drifted down to where he was standing. His head came up and Tao saw the long, curved horns white in the morning sun. In spite of his size Saxon turned quickly, tossing his head, bellowing. Then he charged.

Tao saw him running toward them, snorting and blowing. Quickly Tao grabbed the wolf dog by the scruff of the neck and led him up to the top of the rimrock, a small mound of limestone standing near the edge of the plains. Here they were safe from the great black bull pawing the dust below them.

Tao looked down at the huge bulk of the animal. He saw the play of the powerful muscles under the shiny black hide. He cringed at the sight of the flashing white horns and he saw the angry fire burning in the dark, piercing eyes.

Now Tao understood why this beast had been chosen as the caretaker of tribal laws. Anyone, man or woman, who broke the taboos of the clan was brought up on the high plains to face Saxon, the sacred bull. Given a spear and a flint knife, they were forced to battle this savage brute. If they lived, it was proof that they had done no wrong. None ever did. The scattering of sun-bleached bones lying across the plains told the story.

Tao held Ram tight as the wolf dog growled. "Stay," he said. "We have no quarrel with Saxon. We come only to look." Tao dropped to his knees, studying the powerful beast. Saxon, he thought, you are bigger than I am and you are stronger, but I will capture your image on my stone. He took out a broad flat slate that he had brought with him. Then he sat down on the rimrock, his legs dangling over the edge, and began sketching a picture of the great bull. He tried to catch the heavy body, the strong neck and shoulders and the massive head. His flint tool cut deep, scoring bold white lines on the gray slate.

Saxon grazed alone now, but soon the cows and yearlings would come back and he would once again be lord of the high plains.

When Tao had finished his drawing, he blew off the dust and held up the stone. "Yes," he said to himself, "that is good, that is the beast I want." He looked down at Saxon, then threw back his head and laughed. "Go," he said, "go back to your stomping grounds and wait for your cows. I have your spirit carved on my stone."

Saxon soon grew tired of waiting. He tossed his great head and trotted off across the plains. Tao and Ram climbed down from the rimrock and returned to their little cave. Here Ram lay down in a corner while Tao quickly began copying his picture of the bull. With a piece of yellow clay he made a large outline on the cave wall. Then, studying his sketch, he began drawing line for line, sketching in the muscular shoulders and the deep chest. Next he started the head with its long, curving horns. He drew easily, freely, watching his picture come alive as he filled in the details. It felt good to be working with the smooth, flowing chalk and he forgot to eat.

He was drawing quietly when he heard the wolf dog growl. He looked down to see if Ram was dreaming, but the wolf was wide awake, getting to his feet.

Tao put down his sketch. He could feel sweat break out on his neck. "What is it, Ram?"

The wolf dog went to the entrance, sniffing and growling.

Tao waited, listening. Then he heard the clattering sound of falling dirt and pebbles. His heart beat fast. Someone was climbing up the face of the cliff.

Ram growled again. "Be quiet," whispered Tao.

The sound of climbing continued. Tao looked at his drawing of Saxon on the cave wall. It was the best he had ever done. But quickly he reached down and picked up a handful of soot and moss and rubbed out the image. Then he gathered up all the chalk and charcoal, together with his slate, and hid them under the bearskin robe. He sent Ram to the back of the cave and made him lie down in the darkness.

Silently Tao crept to the entrance and peered out. He saw no one. Yet the sound of falling stones came closer.

The wolf dog whimpered. "Quiet, Ram," Tao repeated. He glanced around the cave. If the climber was Volt or one of the hunters, he would find no trace of drawings or claysticks. The boy pressed himself against the damp wall, gripping his spear tightly. Then he saw fingers reach out, grasping the side of the entrance. It was an old, weathered hand, gnarled and wrinkled. Tao heard a deep hacking cough and he felt a wave of relief. It was Graybeard. A moment later the old man stepped into the mouth of the cave. He was breathing heavily and he leaned back against the wall as he tried to catch his breath.

Ram came out of the darkness and sniffed at the old man's sandals.

"We are happy to see you again," said Tao. "And we are glad you are not one of the hunters."

Graybeard smiled. "I came from above," he said, his voice wheezing. "Only now I find I cannot climb as well as I used to." He stopped again to catch his breath. "I go to the camp of the Mountain People and I thought to stop here for the night."

"We have food and water," said Tao, "and you are always welcome."

The boy put some wood on the fire. They speared chunks of salmon on long sticks and broiled them over the hot flames. They did the same with parts of a duck that Tao had caught the day before. After their meal they ate dried ground plums and drank cockleshells full of birch tea.

When they had finished, Tao picked up the bearskin robe, uncovering the chalk sticks and the sketch of the bull. "I have seen Saxon," he said. "I was drawing his image when you came."

Graybeard looked at the slate stone, studying the sketch. "This image is good," he said. "Now try again and I will watch."

Slowly Tao picked up one of the chalks. His hand shook, and he knew it was because he was working in front of the master. He began to draw, copying from the sketch. He did well with the head and body, but when he came to the legs, his hand would not obey. Once again he felt anger and for a moment he wanted to throw the chalk against the wall.

"You must be patient," said Graybeard. "The eye and the hand will learn to become one. But it takes time." He took the chalk from Tao and dropped it on the floor of the cave. Then he picked up a stick of charcoal and started to draw, showing the boy how to join the legs to the shoulder and hips.

Tao watched closely.

When he had finished, the old man rubbed out the drawing with a handful of moss. He handed the charcoal to Tao. "Now start over," he said. "The black will make a better outline, and this time do not trust your memory but let your hand be guided by the lines on your sketch."

Tao took the charcoal and started again. Line by line he drew another picture of the bull as Graybeard looked on. The old man nodded. "Ah, yes," he said. "That is good. You are learning. Draw as much as you can, but always remember to rub out your pictures when you are through."

"Maybe you will teach me often?" asked Tao. "I will learn more quickly that way."

The old man shook his head gruffly. "You press too hard, boy. I tell you again, you are not a Chosen One. I have already done more than I should."

Tao knew he had angered the old man again. He spoke under his breath. "I did not think you believed in taboos."

But the old man heard him. "That may be," he snapped. "Yet even a shaman must obey the laws of the clan and accept the beliefs of the people." He tugged at his beard. "I have given you permission to draw. I am sorry you do not think that is enough." He rubbed his eyes with the backs of his hands. "Now let us sleep. Tomorrow I have a long way to go."

Tao's face felt hot. He had not meant to, but he had offended the master.

The next morning Graybeard and Tao went out across the valley. The grazing herds of antelope and horses raced away at their approach. They walked all morning and when they came to the river the old man stopped. He looked down at the boy, a thin smile on his lips. "I have changed my mind," he said. "Perhaps the old shaman has become a fool but I will help you."

Tao looked up, his eyes wide.

"Yes," said Graybeard, "I will come back and show you how to draw and paint. I will show you how to mix colors and make brushes. I will tell you how to find firestones and how to read the stars."

Tao was dazed. He hardly knew what to say. "You would show me how to make magic?"

"Yes, and that too. But you must use it for good, never for evil."

Tao nodded. "Only for good," he said.

"Then I will show you. But I cannot tell you that you will ever be a Chosen One."

Tao felt a warm glow of hope. Never did he think that such good fortune would be his.

"We must do this thing in secret," said Graybeard. "I will find a hidden place. Then you and Ram will come."

"When?" asked Tao. "Where will this place be?"

The old man shook his head, frowning again. "You must not push so hard. Have patience. When I am ready I will let you know."

"But how will I find you?"

"By magic," said Graybeard, his blue eyes shining.

Tao did not wish to anger the old man again. Yet he did not want to lose this chance. "And I will know the magic?"

Graybeard smiled. "When the time is right you will know."

"But—?"

The old man held up his hand. "No more questions now. I have a long journey. I will go downstream and cross the river at the shallows. There you cannot follow."

Graybeard walked away hunched over, coughing badly. Tao watched him disappear through the trees. He knelt down and threw his arm around the wolf dog's shoulder. "Think of it, Ram. Soon I will be a true image maker."

▪ TEN

A full moon passed and another began and it was almost summer.

Whenever Tao left the little cave to go hunting with Ram, he looked out over the valley to be sure that Volt or Garth and the other hunters were not around. Now he looked across the verdant grassland, warm and bright in the early morning sunlight. He saw noisy flocks of dusty brown linnets fly over the meadows, settling at times to rest and feed, then rising up again like a tawny cloud.

Small bands of horses grazed alongside saiga antelopes as they wandered across the open fields. But this morning Tao saw no man, no hunter. Everything seemed quiet and at peace.

Then he saw something far off in the distance. He strained his eyes but he could make it out only as a long line of great brown bodies, moving slowly. It came out of the bottomlands, along the river, rolling ponderously onto the plains.

Tao knew it was a vast herd of animals. But he could not yet see it clearly. Sometimes it was hidden by a white haze of dust that hovered over it, moving along with it. Then it came into view again, a living thing winding its way along. It was still far away, but it was getting closer.

Tao held his hand up to his forehead, shielding his eyes from the sun. He looked again. He gasped and felt his heart leap. "They're here, Ram," he cried. "The mountains-that-walk have come back."

He picked up his spear and went down the cliff, stumbling, sliding to the bottom with Ram close behind him. Without stopping they ran out across the valley, racing through the knee-high grass, scattering the game before them. The antelopes went bounding away; the horses whinnied and galloped off.

Breathing heavily, the boy and the wolf dog plunged headlong into the swamps. Here they would be downwind from the animals. They could hide in the tall reed grass and watch in safety.

Standing in the shallow water, they waited silently as the first groups of mammoths lumbered into the open meadow. Tao pushed aside the reeds to get a better view. He could see the herd clearly now. It was made up of cows, with many yearlings and calves. As tall as the birch trees, some of the older, elephantlike animals had long, sweeping tusks that curved inward, almost crossing over at the ends. Thick, hanging mats of reddish-brown hair covered their bodies, all shaggy and disheveled from late spring shedding.

The calves wandered on either side of the herd, exploring, romping, then running back. Great black-winged vultures soared overhead, circling the herd.

Tao counted on his fingers. It was three summers since the mountains-that-walk had come through the valley. Now they were back and Tao was overwhelmed at the sight of them. Of all the animals in the valley, he loved to watch the mountains-that-walk best. They were like the earth, massive, shaggy old giants, lumbering out of the dawn.

Moving slowly, in scattered groups, the monsters plodded along, pulling up great trunkfuls of grass, bending down the willows and birch trees to get at the succulent buds and twigs.

Tao was still downwind from the animals. Never had he seen so many, never had he been so near to the gigantic beasts. They were so close he could hear the gurgling rumble of their stomachs. He could smell the musty odor of their bodies and see the clouds of blackflies buzzing around their heads.

Ram's eyes followed the slow-moving giants, a low, guttural growl coming from deep within his throat. The boy held him tight by the scruff of the neck, and the wolf dog strained until his breathing was almost choked. Tao could feel Ram's body tremble with excitement. "No, Ram," he whispered.

"They are too big. You would have no chance against the monsters."

The mammoths kept coming and coming, and now they seemed to be everywhere. Then Tao heard sounds behind him, sounds of breaking reeds and sloshing water, sounds of heavy bodies splashing through the swamp. He was no longer downwind. He was no longer safe. They were all around him.

Suddenly one of the lead cows caught the man scent and sounded the alarm. Long, snakelike trunks swept overhead, searching for the danger. Trumpeting shrieks filled the air. Hurriedly the calves and yearlings moved into the center of the herd.

The shrieks and squeals and the thundering bodies were everywhere.

Ram tugged and squirmed, and before Tao could stop him he pulled away and dashed straight into the milling herd.

"Stop, Ram, stop!" Tao shouted. But it was too late. Already the wolf dog was leaping and snapping at the legs of the nearest beast.

Tao cried out, shouting again and again, trying to make himself heard. But his voice was drowned out by pounding feet and wild screams. He stood by helplessly as he saw the wolf dog dart from one angry animal to another, dashing between them, nipping at their legs.

With amazing quickness the big animals whirled around, lashing out, striking back at this annoying pest. Two or three times Tao saw Ram disappear

nto a jumble of legs and trunks, any minute expect-
ng him to be thrown into the air or impaled on a
ong, curved tusk. Once the wolf dog was caught by a
swinging trunk and sent sprawling into the swamp-
grass. But Ram was quick. He leaped to his feet and
charged again, snapping, jumping, dodging out of
he way, almost toying with the enraged beasts as
he boy looked on in horror.

Noises filled the swamp, reeds cracked. The great
beasts were crashing through. Tao could feel the
earth shake. Wild trumpeting filled his ears and he
heard the slogging footsteps behind him. Slowly he
started to back out of the swamp. But the reed grass
grew high overhead and he could not see the angry
monsters floundering all around him. He could only
hear them, sloshing through the water, coming
closer and closer. He waited silently, hoping they
would turn back or go on their way. But the sounds
only grew louder. One step at a time he backed away
through the tall grass as the plodding beasts came
in. With a sinking feeling, he realized that one of the
big cows was following him. Tao stood perfectly still,
listening to the heavy footsteps and the pounding of
his heart. She's there, he thought, and she knows I
m waiting.

Then he saw the reeds bend and crack and he
heard the splash of water as the animal broke
through the tall grass. A huge cow loomed up over
him, standing like a dark shadow, water dripping
from her long, reddish-brown hair. Tao's eyes were

wide with fright. She was much bigger than he ex
pected. Her great shaggy head hung over him, sharp
curving tusks glistened in the sunlight. She lifted he
trunk and let out an ear-splitting scream of anger.

Tao whirled around. There was no place to run. H
stepped back, recklessly trying to force his wa
through the reeds. The jagged edges scratched hi
bare arms. For a long moment the monster towere
over him, a low, rumbling growl coming from dee
within her chest.

The boy stumbled backward, falling into the reed
He got up quickly, dripping swampwater from hi
arms and face. At that moment the mammot
charged. With a wild shriek she lunged at him
stomping, splashing through the water, kicking u
showers of slime and mud.

Tao dropped his spear. He threw up his arms t
protect his face as the hairy giant came on. A lor
trunk reached out and gripped him around th
waist. It lifted him bodily up into the air, then thre
him crashing into the reed grass.

With the wind knocked out of him, Tao lay in th
murky water, trying to catch his breath. He fe
stabs of pain. His arms and legs were cut and blee
ing. Slowly he rolled over on his back as the sta
nant water washed about his shoulders. He looke
up and saw the tops of the reed grass waving ove
head. He started to get up. Then, with a feeling
awesome terror, he saw the great beast standi
above him. Her legs were like hairy logs as she lift

one giant foot and held it over him. She started to bring it down.

Tao rolled out of the way, just as the foot splashed in the water beside him. But the angry brute lifted her foot again. Tao looked up at the cracked leathery sole about to come down on his head.

Just then he saw a flash of gray fur plunge into the reeds. It was Ram, flinging himself at the raging mammoth. He badgered her, harassed her, nipping at her legs. She spun around, lashing back at him, but Ram leaped and dodged, staying clear of her swinging trunk.

Tao lay still for a moment, his eyes wide with fear. Slowly he started to get up, his fingers groping for his spear. Just as he got to his feet the mammoth turned again to face him. With a loud shriek she started to charge.

But the great beast never reached him. Out of the corner of her eye she saw the wolf dog chasing her calf, which had come up behind her. Instantly, she whirled around and went crashing through the reeds after them.

Mud-spattered and tired, Tao stood in the tall reeds, waiting, listening, afraid to move. Slowly the sounds of the thundering herd rumbled off into the distance. When he was sure it was safe, Tao began washing the dirt and mud from his arms and legs, still bleeding from the cuts and scratches of the sharp reed grass. Painfully he limped out of the swamp. In the distance he could see a rising cloud of dust and he knew the great herd had re-formed and was continuing on its way.

With an uneasy feeling Tao followed the tracks of the wandering beasts, hoping he would not find Ram trampled in the dust. He had not gone far when he saw the wolf dog loping toward him through the meadow, his sides heaving, his tongue hanging. He was wet, his gray coat caked with mud. Tao threw his arms around the animal's neck, burying his face in the wet fur. "You are brave, Ram," he said, "but you are foolish. The mammoths are not rabbits. They are dangerous."

Ram's eyes were bright and he was panting heavily from his wild run.

"This time I was lucky," said Tao. "You saved my life. Never again will I let you chase the mountains-that-walk."

▪ ELEVEN

Tao's cuts and bruises were painful but not serious. Kala gave him plantain leaves and a poultice made of earth apple to put on his wounds. She also gave him a sackful of chestnuts to boost his spirits.

Tao smiled at her. "It has been a long time since I have had one of these."

Kala shook her old gray head. "If you go on chasing the mammoths, you will not live long enough to eat them."

Summer came and a bright sun filled the valley with its warm glow. Tao watched the golden eagles soaring on the warm updrafts, their sharp eyes searching for rabbits and marmots. The antelopes now shared the valley with herds of small, shaggy ponies or tarpans not much bigger than a wolf dog.

One afternoon as Tao was coming back from the Slough with Ram, he looked up to see a rainbow of colors rippling across the white cliffs. Splashes of yellow gave way to blues, then purple, as the sun moved in and out of the clouds.

Then, suddenly, he saw a bright flash of white light come from the top of the limestone cliff. For a moment it danced and flickered in the sunshine. Tao shook his head, puzzled, wondering what would make such a strange light. A moment later he saw it again. It sparkled and shone like a star, beckoning him.

He walked across the open field, and each time he saw it he stopped and tried to think where he had seen that light before. When he reached the foot of the cliffs, he stood quietly watching it as it flashed on and off in the sunlight. Then, all at once, it came back to him and he knew what it was. It was the shining stone.

A broad smile crossed his face. He forgot about everything else and started to run. "Come, Ram," he shouted, pointing to the top of the cliffs. "It is our good friend Graybeard. He is making his magic."

Halfway up the cliff, Tao stopped at his little cave. There he tied his spear over his shoulder with a leather thong. He picked up the bag of chestnuts and tucked it under his belt. Then he started to climb as Ram followed. They went up a narrow, winding ledge, picking their way over jumbles of loose rock and stones.

Soon the path became steeper. Tao reached out, grasping the stunted pine shrubs that grew from the crevices along the rock wall. He stepped on jutting rocks and his fingers felt for cracks and crannies to pull himself up.

Ram was a good climber, but at some places his paws slipped and scraped on the uneven surface. Once Tao helped him around an overhang, and twice he had to pull him up by the scruff of the neck. Frequently they stopped to rest and, little by little, they made their way up the steep limestone wall.

As they came closer, Tao saw Graybeard's wrinkled face looking down over the edge of the cliff. He wondered how the old man had made such a difficult climb.

Breathing hard, Tao pushed Ram over the top, then pulled himself up the rest of the way. Graybeard reached down with a bony hand and helped the boy to his feet. He was smiling broadly. "You saw the light from far off and you knew it was the shining stone?"

"Yes," said Tao, glancing into the old man's blue eyes. "Your magic is good. But it is a hard climb even for a boy."

"That is why I chose this place," said Graybeard. "But there is an easier way. I will show you later." He led Tao over to a clump of bushes. There the old man removed a covering of pine branches to reveal a small opening leading underground.

"It is well hidden," said the old man. "No one will find us here."

They followed a narrow tunnel down to a cavern

where shafts of sunlight filtered through from above. Tao saw the unmarked walls and the high, arched roof. On the floor were sticks of charcoal together with chunks of dried clay. A surge of excitement raced through him and he felt a new wave of joy. To become an image maker was the thing he had always dreamed of. To be taught by the master was more than he had ever hoped for. "My hands and my eyes are ready to begin," he said.

"Ah, my friend, do not be in such a hurry." The old man bent over, stifling a cough. Then he continued. "You will be a better pupil after we have eaten."

Tao forced a smile. Food meant nothing to him now. But he did not wish to press the old man. He took the bag of chestnuts from his belt and handed it to Graybeard. "Kala gave me these," he said. "I have been saving them for you."

Graybeard opened the skin sack and peered in. He took out one of the shiny red nuts and held it up in his thin fingers, smiling. "Chestnuts are not plentiful," he said. "It will be good to taste them again."

They sat on the floor of the cave and ate part of a roasted antelope leg that Graybeard had brought with him. They roasted the chestnuts and cracked them open between two stones and picked out the sweet meat. Ram gnawed at the leg bone which still had some meat on it, then curled up in a corner and went to sleep.

Bright sunlight came through the opening and reflected off the ash-gray walls of the cavern.

Graybeard got to his feet. He lifted his thin arms over his head and stretched. Then he looked down at the boy. "Now it is time to begin," he said.

He took a slate stone from his deerskin pouch. "When we were together before, I showed you how to rough out your image, how to draw a bison. Now you must try something harder." He handed Tao the stone.

Tao took it and studied the carved engraving. It was the figure of a reindeer with branching antlers and long, thin legs. He knew it would not be easy. He picked up one of the chalks and stepped to the wall. It was clean and unmarked and he ran the palm of his hand over the surface, feeling the smoothness of it. Then he lifted his other hand and made the first bold strokes, starting with the shoulder and back.

The old man stopped him immediately, shaking his head briskly. "That is wrong. I have told you, always make your first sketch in charcoal. Black is better. And start with an outline of the body and the head."

Tao groaned inwardly. In his excitement he had already forgotten the first lesson the old man had taught him. He picked up a stick of charcoal and began again.

The old master watched for a while, then reached out and stopped the boy's hand again. "No," he said sharply. "You draw with short, choppy strokes. Let your hand go free. Let it glide over the wall. There is plenty of room, reach out as far as you can."

As he followed Graybeard's instructions Tao found he was drawing easier, faster. He smiled with a quick feeling of satisfaction. Just a few words from the master made a big difference.

Graybeard nodded. "You are learning, my friend. It takes time, but you are learning."

Tao drew the outline of two more reindeer before the old man stopped him again. "Now I will show you something else," said Graybeard. He took another graven stone from his leather pouch and handed it to Tao. On it was the sketch of a rhino. Then he brushed his long fingers across the wall. "Look, here," he said. "When you draw the rhino, use this bulge as the high part of the back. The hollow place below it then becomes the dark area where the head meets the shoulder."

Tao did as he was told, outlining a large rhino. When he had finished, he stepped back, his dark eyes wide with wonder. "Look," he said, "it begins to live."

Graybeard picked up the charcoal. "Now, if you wish to show many animals together, you outline the first one, then draw a row of heads and legs, one after another." Graybeard sketched a bison on the wall, then drew a series of heads and legs close behind it.

Again Tao was surprised. With a few quick strokes the old master had created an entire herd of bison. He could almost see the flashing eyes and hear the pounding hooves. "It is magic," he said. "Now I will try."

The old man shook his head. He walked about the little cavern, stretching his arms over his head. "That is enough for now. Tomorrow I must go to the camp of the Lake People. When I return, I will show you how to paint and mix colors. For that we will need some fish oil, some animal fat and blood and some eggs and honey."

The following morning Graybeard took Tao west, along the top of the cliffs, until they came to a narrow path leading down to the bottom. "It is not so steep," said the old man, "and much easier to climb."

They walked across the valley until they came to the river. When they were ready to part, the boy said, "Thank you, Graybeard. I will work hard to make the bison live on the cave wall. Then someday maybe I will be nearly as good as you are."

The old man smiled, tugging at his beard. "Maybe better," he said.

"No one can be better. But I will try."

The old man walked away, coughing heavily. Tao called after him. "You will be back soon?"

"Do not be impatient," said Graybeard. Tao caught the flicker of a smile. "You have enough to do while I am gone."

In the days that followed, Tao practiced his drawings. In between he collected materials for the next lesson. He searched along the dry streambeds for saucer-shaped stones that could be used to mix paints. He scooped wet clay out of the brook and wrapped it in fresh green leaves to keep it moist and soft.

Down at the Slough he caught two big fat carp and brought them back to his cave, where he baked them over an open fire and squeezed out the oil. Kala gave him a large seashell, three duck eggs and a jackal skull full of honey. When everything was ready he stored them in the Hidden Cave at the top of the cliff to wait for Graybeard's return.

They still needed some animal fat and blood, and one day, near the edge of the swamp, Ram picked up the scent of a boar. He tracked it into the spruce forest, where he brought it to bay in the middle of a berry thicket. It fought viciously, twisting and lashing out with its tusks. Tao threw his spear with all his strength. The boar squealed and thrashed about, then lay still.

After he skinned the animal, Tao scraped out much of the fat and collected some of the blood in a hollow bone. He cut off the head and the best parts of the meat and tied it together in the skin and brought it back to the Hidden Cave. There he stored the blood and fat away, to be used for the mixing of the paints. The meat and the rest of the animal he brought back to Kala and the clan people.

Soon the odor of roast pig drifted through the little camp as the women speared the legs and ribs on spits and turned them over the open fires. The people were pleased, for it was not often that they were treated to such tasty fare.

Even Volt was more friendly. He gave Tao the tusks from the boar's skull to wear around his neck as an amulet and as a token of his hunting skill.

Tao was happy to please Volt, and even Garth. He wished he could tell Volt about Ram and how the wolf dog could hunt. But he knew the leader would not listen, so he held his tongue. Yet he wished that someday Ram could show his worth in front of the entire clan. Then maybe Volt would know the wolf dog was not an evil spirit.

■ TWELVE

With Graybeard gone, Tao felt a new sense of emptiness. He spent much of his time drawing mammoths, bison and rhinos in Graybeard's little cavern. Each evening he stood on top of the cliff, scanning the valley, waiting for the old man to return. As the days passed and Graybeard did not show up, the boy became impatient. Why does he not come back? he thought. He has always kept his word. Maybe something is wrong. He considered going to find him, but he knew he could not cross the river or go into the lands of the other people.

Each day the boy waited with growing concern. Then, one morning, down in the Slough, Ram growled and Tao looked up to see Graybeard standing in the middle of the glade as if he had come out of the earth. He had his flint-tipped spear in his hand and he carried the shoulder blade of a horse strapped to his back.

Tao hurried toward him, an expression of joy and relief in his eyes. "I am happy to see you, old shaman. It has been a long time."

Graybeard nodded. "There are many places I must go, and I do not walk as fast as I used to." The old man coughed and passed a shaky hand across his brow.

Tao winced as he saw the worn face, the pinched cheekbones. He was worried, but he knew the old man would not want him to show concern. "The cave is ready," Tao said. "But first you must rest and eat." He took some dried meat and fish from his leather pouch and they sat with their backs against an old red oak and ate their meal. Tao wondered if Graybeard remembered his promise.

When they were finished, they started across the valley. Graybeard stopped many times, poking around the streambeds and gravel banks with the shaft of his spear, searching. Then he found what he was looking for. He picked up a stick and dug out a handful of bright red earth.

"Here," he said, as he poured it into an empty leather sack. "This will make good red paint. Now we must find yellows and whites."

"I have yellow clay," said Tao. The old man did remember.

"Good. We can dig up some limestone powder

near the foot of the cliffs. That will mix well for the lighter colors."

When they had all the red, white and yellow earth they needed, they went up to the top of the cliff, using the easy path that Graybeard had found. They reached the tunnel to the Hidden Cave and removed the cover of branches to let in the sunlight.

In the cave Graybeard sat on the ground and Tao squatted beside him. The old man poured some of the red earth into one of the saucer-shaped rocks that Tao had collected. Then, using a smooth, round stone, he began grinding it into a fine powder. When it was to his liking, he added some of Tao's fish oil, mixing it into a dark red paint. He poured a small amount of this into three other shallow stone dishes. In the first one he added a lump of yellow clay, in the second he sprinkled limestone powder and in the third he added charcoal dust. Using a small, clean stick for each, he mixed them well, ending with three different colors: a bright orange, a salmon pink and a dark brown.

Tao was amazed. He sat quietly, watching. This too was magic, he thought. Graybeard spread out more saucers and began blending shades of yellows, browns, grays and blacks. Some he mixed with honey, and some with the boiled fat and clotted blood from the boar.

"Next we must make our brushes," he said. He took a handful of twigs from his pouch and began mashing the ends with a stone until they were soft and ragged. He held one up in the shaft of sunlight beaming through the cave entrance. He turned it around for Tao to see. "These are small," he said, "for painting eyes and fine lines of hair and fur."

He made larger brushes by tying feathers and boar bristles around the ends of long sticks with strings of vegetable fiber.

When all the paints and brushes were made, the old man got to his feet. "Now," he said, "we are ready to paint."

Tao held out the shoulder blade of the horse, while Graybeard poured spots of the colored paints onto its broad white surface. He handed the boy one of the large brushes and pointed to Tao's pictures of the rhinos, bison and mammoths.

The boy held his breath. He had never had a brush in his hand before. "Which one will I paint?"

Graybeard smiled. "You are the image maker. Paint the one you like the best."

"The mountain-that-walks," said Tao.

Graybeard nodded. "Then begin."

Tao hesitated, glancing at the paints on the shoulder blade, uncertain.

"You saw the mammoths," said Graybeard. "What color were they?"

"Reddish-brown."

"Good," said the old man. "Then mix a little black with the red until you have the color you wish."

Tao dipped his brush into the spot of black, then mixed it with the red. He lifted his hand and touched it to the drawing. It was still too light, so he dipped in another dab of black. Again his brush touched the drawing. He smiled. It was a deep reddish-brown, the color he wanted. He continued to dip and touch.

Graybeard watched as Tao repeated the motion again and again. He reached out and stopped the boy's hand. "You are not painting on an antler or a seashell," he said. "You are painting on a wall. Do not dab. Swing the brush with your whole arm."

Graybeard took the brush and began sweeping it across the drawing, following the lines of the mammoth's body.

Tao saw the old man's face brighten as he worked, laying on great swaths of color. He felt the excitement as the picture came alive.

"Do not be afraid," said Graybeard, his eyes glowing. "You can always go over what you do not like."

He gave the brush back to Tao and the boy tried again. This time he let his arm go free, swinging the brush across the wall. He mixed gray with yellow to fill in the light areas around the chest and stomach. He painted dark shadows on the shoulders and back to add shading. He saw his mammoth begin to breathe as he filled in the eye and the waving trunk.

When the painting was finished, Graybeard cracked open the duck eggs. He separated the yolks and set them aside. He poured the whites into a clean cockleshell, stirred them with a stick and handed the shell to Tao.

The boy was puzzled. "What is this for?"

"Spread it over your painting and you will see."

With a feather brush Tao washed the egg white over the picture. This time the mammoth came alive with bright new colors. He stared at it in surprise. This had been done by his own hand. He smiled. Never had he felt so happy.

The following morning Graybeard went off on his mission of mercy and magic. He was gone for long periods, but he always returned to the little cavern at the top of the cliff to show the boy more about the painting, how to make light and shadows, where to find the red and yellow earth with which to make colors. Sometimes they sat together, on the edge of the cliffs, talking. Here they looked up at the night sky and Graybeard pointed out the stars, the first one to appear each night, the one that was red and the one that always leads toward the north. Here too Graybeard showed him how to make fire and told him where to find the special herbs to cure sickness.

The last time the old man went off on his journey, Tao and Ram walked with him across the valley. When they reached the river, Graybeard turned. "Your drawings are better now, they are true and they begin to live. Maybe now you can call yourself a cave painter."

"I thank you for that," said Tao. "And for all the things you have taught me. I am happy."

The old man smiled. "You know the many beautiful things you can make with a brush and a dab of paint. That is all you have to know. That is all that really matters."

They said good-bye, and as the old man walked away, Tao heard the long, hacking cough. He noticed the weary, shambling gait. His heart ached and deep inside he was afraid for his old friend.

▪ THIRTEEN

One afternoon Tao and Ram were up in the mountains, above the treeline, hunting ptarmigan. They were on their way down when Tao looked below to see Volt and the clan hunters stalking a herd of red deer through the spruce forest. The herd was made up of two does, with fawns, together with a few yearlings. Tao counted them on his fingers. There were nine in all.

The wolf dog was eager to attack, but the boy held him back. They watched quietly from a distance as the hunters formed a large circle surrounding the unwary animals.

If Tao could only get close enough for Ram to run in and pull down one of the deer, it would show how well the wolf dog could hunt. Cautiously he led Ram down to the edge of the spruce wood as the hunters moved silently through the trees, getting ready to throw their spears.

Unaware of the approaching danger, the deer grazed peacefully on moss and lichen. Tao's heart raced as the hunters crept closer to the unsuspecting deer. If he let the wolf dog go too soon, it would spook the animals and they would get away.

He moved silently, slowly, trying to get as close as possible. Even if Ram could not catch one of the animals, he might be able to drive them into the spears of the waiting hunters. Tao knew it would have to be done at just the right moment.

The wolf dog was ready to spring, and the boy could feel the tension in his body. In the middle of the wood the deer were still browsing quietly. The hunters moved like leopard cats, slowly closing the circle.

At that moment Tao saw a full-grown doe near the edge of the herd. Tall and chestnut-brown, she was the leader of the herd, and her black liquid eyes were alert, searching for danger. Ram could easily reach her within a few strides. But Tao waited. It was still too soon. "Stay," he whispered.

The wolf dog's body trembled under Tao's hold as Ram strained to pull away. Still Tao waited.

Then he saw the big doe flinch. Her head came up and she sniffed the air. If she stamped and gave the alarm, the entire herd would disappear like the wind. He saw her body stiffen as she sensed danger, and Tao could wait no longer. With a quick nudge he pushed Ram ahead. "Now," he whispered. "Go."

The wolf dog dashed out, running straight for the deer. With great bounding leaps, he raced between

the spruce trees and passed through the ring of hunters, closing on his prey.

The doe stamped and turned quickly, springing
into the air. With a single leap she spun around. For
a flickering moment both animals were blurred into
one and Tao was sure the wolf dog had made his kill.
But when he looked again, he saw the big doe
bounding away in the opposite direction. Quickly
Ram swerved to cut her off. It was too late. The deer
was already strides ahead of him.

Tao groaned as he saw the rest of the herd scatter
and all of the deer escape through the ring of hunters. In his excitement he had let Ram go too quickly.
He heard the hunters grumbling and cursing, staring
after the fleeing deer.

Tao stood at the edge of the spruce wood, a sinking
feeling in his heart as he saw Ram come loping
through the trees. Then he saw Garth jump out of
the underbrush directly in the wolf dog's path,
threatening him with his spear.

Ram crouched on the forest floor, his slitted eyes
staring up at the leader, the hair along his back bristling.

"Ghost of evil," roared Volt, stalking up behind
Garth. "Scourge of demons. I will cut out your black
heart!"

Tao knew neither Volt nor Garth had seen him yet,
and for one awful moment he waited in the shadows.
Then he saw Volt raise his arm. With all his strength
he hurled the spear straight at the crouching animal.

But Tao was already vaulting through the air,

throwing himself between Ram and the flying spear. His hand struck the wooden shaft of the weapon, knocking it to the ground.

Volt spun around. He looked at Tao, then at the wolf dog, then back at Tao again, a puzzled expression on his face. Then slowly Volt began to understand, and a burning fury filled his dark eyes. "Pah!" he cried, almost spitting out the word. "So this is how you hunt alone? You and this evil beast are one."

"No," said Tao, trying to explain. "The wolf dog is not bad. He is no evil demon. He is a good hunter . . . he . . . he has helped me bring much game to the clan people."

The big man scowled darkly, shaking his woolly head. "No," he sneered. "This beast is the soul of a devil and you call him friend." He reached up and rubbed the scars on his cheek with the back of his hand. "This demon and his kind have haunted me all my life, and I will kill every last one of them."

Garth stepped toward Tao, frowning, but Volt had already turned toward the woods. "Come," he shouted to the hunters. "Help me kill this evil spirit and rid me of this curse."

As Volt and Garth watched over the wolf dog, Tao crept into the nearby spruce trees.

Tao heard the hunters coming. He knew there was no use in pleading for Ram's life. Volt would not listen, the hunters would not care. Suddenly he jumped away, shouting, "Come, Ram. Come!" The wolf dog sprang between the waiting men, racing after Tao, down through the spruce wood and out across the open meadow. Tao did not look back, but he could hear the cries and shouts as the angry men followed.

Dodging, turning, lurching through the tall grass, boy and wolf barely managed to keep ahead of their pursuers. Slipping through the birch stands, plunging through the high swamp grass, they raced for the Slough.

Halfway there Tao saw some of the hunters running to cut him off. His heart sank. That route of escape was blocked. He would have to head for the river.

Quickly he changed direction, leaping over the winding brooks. The bushes and trees became a blur of green, the ground sped away beneath him. He ran through the edge of the oak forest, vaulting along on his spear. His arms grew tired. If only he could stop to hide, to rest and take a quiet breath.

Then he caught a whiff of smoke. He looked back and saw tongues of yellow flame licking up into the sky. The hunters had started a grass fire to keep him from doubling back.

He ran straight ahead and reached the river, stopping under the branches of a giant willow tree. Here he looked around, breathing heavily. The river was an invisible wall. On the far side was the land of the Mountain People. For moments he paced the muddy bank with Ram, trying to make up his mind.

Then he heard the shouts of the hunters. They were racing ahead of the fire, getting closer. On the other side of the river the wolf dog would be safe. The hunters would not follow. He looked down at Ram. "You must go across the river," he said. "Stay there until I call."

Ram looked up, whining.

Tao pointed to the other shore. "Go," he said, pushing the wolf dog into the water. Once, twice, Ram turned back, but Tao kept pushing him into the water. "Go," he said sternly. "Go now." He threw stones and sticks, chasing the wolf dog further and further out into the river.

Soon Ram was swimming. Tao saw his head bobbing on the water as the current carried him downstream. He watched as the wolf dog pulled himself up on the opposite shore and shook himself off. He saw him look back once or twice, then disappear into the trees.

A moment later the hunters came crashing through the underbrush.

■ FOURTEEN

When he heard the hunters coming through the woods, Tao jumped behind the big willow tree. He looked around quickly. There was no place else to hide. He was breathing hard and he was too tired to start running again. Then he glanced up into the branches of the willow, with its thick canopy of new green leaves.

With a wild throw he hurled his spear into a thicket of thornbushes, then started up the tree. The massive trunk was growing at a rakish angle and he had little trouble climbing up through the branches. High above the ground, he stretched himself out on a heavy limb, the way he had seen the leopard cats do. He peered down through the curtain of leaves, scarcely daring to breathe.

The smell of smoke still hung in the air, but as he looked back across the valley he saw that the fire had nearly burned itself out.

He had barely settled himself on his rough perch when the hunters came swarming around the foot of the tree. They grunted and shouted and pointed toward the river. They searched around the clumps of thornbushes and followed the footprints up and down the riverbank.

A moment later Tao saw Volt come into the clearing. The big leader soon found the spear in the thicket. He held it up and showed it to the hunters. Tao was certain they must know he was not far away.

He watched as Garth came up and went with Volt down by the river. He could hear them talking and wading through the shallow water, studying the tracks of the wolf dog on the bank.

The big leader walked back under the willow tree. He stood there looking around, grunting and shaking the spear as Garth and the other hunters searched the bank. Then, slowly, he glanced up into the branches of the willow. Tao held his breath. He pressed his body against the rough bark and felt it dig into his arms and legs. Cautiously he peered down through the screen of branches and leaves. Volt was still directly below. The big man walked around the tree. He kept looking up, scanning the branches. Then he stopped and looked straight at Tao. For one brief moment their eyes met. The boy was sure he had been discovered. He waited silently, his heart pounding, as he dug his fingers into the gray bark.

Volt continued to walk beneath the tree, his eyes searching from branch to branch. With a wave of relief Tao saw him turn away and go down to the river, where he joined the other hunters. There Volt held up the boy's spear and shook it over his head again. "The fools have crossed the river," he shouted.

Garth grunted. "Let the Mountain People find them."

The hunters mumbled to each other and nodded in agreement.

Volt shook his fist. "Come," he said, pointing his spear toward camp. "Let us go back."

Tao stayed up on his hidden perch. He was sure Volt must have seen him. Calling off the hunters might only be a trick to get him down. He waited grimly for darkness. Then he climbed to the ground, cramped from his long watch. Bone tired, he spent the night huddled in the shadows of the riverbank, thinking about Ram. In a few days, if the hunters did not return, he would call the wolf dog back.

The next morning, still tired and hungry, Tao fished for minnows in the pools and eddies along the riverbank. He had only caught a few when he heard an eerie drawn-out howl come from across the water. It was a long, mournful *whooo-woo-woo-woo* and it drifted over on the misty morning air. It came again and again, echoing through the dank woodlands. The boy listened for a few moments, wondering. He heard it again, louder this time.

Suddenly his body stiffened. It was the howl of a wolf.

Tao walked up and down along the riverbank, looking toward the far side, where the mountain sloped down to the water and the hemlock and spruce trees crowded the shore. Again he listened and again he heard the sad, lonely cry. Without waiting longer, he pulled off his deerskin boots, tucked them under his belt and plunged into the river. He swam steadily, his dark head bobbing above the cold water. The swift current carried him downstream as he made for the opposite shore. When he got close to the bank, he reached out and grabbed an overhanging hemlock branch and pulled himself out of the water. Stepping onto the dry land, he sat down and shoved his feet into the wet boots. He found a broken tree limb and, using it as a crutch, he vaulted up through the woods.

The howling continued, coming from somewhere on the distant hillside. Tao made his way up through the spruce forest, hobbling over the stones and roots, guided by the wailing howl. Desperately he pushed through the tangle of undergrowth. All he could think of was Ram.

He saw fresh tracks going up the steep slope, and he knew men had been this way only a short time before.

He plunged through a low stand of hemlocks, ducking under the branches, tripping on the creepers. The howling cries were closer now. Suddenly he

rashed through a thicket of junipers and stepped
nto a clearing. There was Ram, lying on the ground,
lone, his legs lashed to a pole with leather thongs.
Vhen he saw the boy, the wolf dog whined and
truggled to get free.

Tao's anger flared. He ran up to the wolf dog and
ut his hand on the animal's shoulder. "Hold still,"
e whispered as he drew his flint knife and began to
ut the bindings. Ram squirmed. Tao was almost fin-
hed when a heavy voice called out, "Let the wolf
og be."

The boy whirled around to see a large, red-
earded man dressed in a bearskin robe step out of
ie bushes. The big man glared at him. He held a
pear, pointing it at Tao. The boy heard the sound of
otsteps and snapping twigs. A moment later, nine
iore hunters came out of the underbrush. They
ere dressed in sheepskin tunics, and all of them
arried spears. Tao saw the anger in their eyes.
Who are you?" asked the red-haired leader. He
oke a language almost like Tao's own.

"I am Tao of the Valley People."

The man grunted. He understood. "We have
atched you across the river with your wolf dog.
ow you hunt on our land."

"No," said Tao. "I came only to get Ram. I do not
ant your game."

The big leader shook his head, his eyes flashing de-
ance. "The wolf dog stays," he said. "He belongs to
; now."

Tao's fist tightened around his flint knife and he stepped forward. Two of the hunters grabbed him by the arms and held him back. The others tied Ram's mouth with fibers and thongs, then lifted him up on the long pole. The wolf dog squirmed and struggled, froth dripping from his mouth as he tried to get free.

Tao twisted and tried to pull away. Anger surged through him as he saw the hunters carry Ram into the forest. "Let the wolf dog go," he said harshly. "He has done you no harm. I will leave your land. I will never return."

Once again the man shook his head.

"Then give me the wolf dog," said Tao. "I will hunt with him ... here ... and bring you much food."

The big leader glanced at the hunters, looking from one to another. They shook their heads. But one said, "Maybe the boy speaks wisely. It will be a help to have a wolf dog again."

The leader grunted. "Come," he said, "bring the boy. We will ask the shaman."

Tao turned quickly. "You have the shaman?"

"Yes," said the leader. "He rests in our camp."

"Graybeard?"

The big man nodded as he strode ahead. "He is sick."

Tao followed the hunters up through the pine forest to the camp of the Mountain People, where a circle of skin huts was set up at the foot of the high

dge. Three women were busy skinning an ibex
while children played with stones near a woodpile.
They stopped and looked up, their dark eyes full of
curiosity, as Tao limped into the clearing.

The red-bearded leader took him over to one of the
huts, where he reached down and opened the skin
flap. "Here," he said. "The shaman sleeps. He does
not eat and he grows thin."

In the dim light Tao saw Graybeard lying on a bed
of dried grass and skins. The old man lifted his head
slowly, his sunken eyes blinking from the light. A
spasm of coughs racked his body as he crawled out
of the hut.

Tao was shocked. He had never seen the old man
so thin and feeble.

"Ah," said Graybeard, his voice weak. "The Mountain People have brought you? They say I am dying."

The boy shook his head. He looked up at the red-
bearded leader, unwilling to believe what he had
heard. "It cannot be." Tao knelt. "Graybeard, with
rest you will be well again."

"Perhaps," said Graybeard, "but first you must
help me get back to the land of your people."

Tao shook his head again. "I cannot go back."

"Why?"

The leader looked down. "Tell the shaman."

Tao looked uneasily at the man, then began. He
told Graybeard how he had sent Ram across the
river to escape Volt and the clan hunters and how
the Mountain People had captured him.

The big leader nodded. "Now he will stay with u
and hunt with the wolf dog."

"No," said Graybeard. He cannot stay."

The leader scowled and went away.

"Do not worry," said Graybeard to Tao. "I will te
them to let the wolf dog go."

"But if I take Ram back to the valley, my peopl
will kill him."

Graybeard held up a hand. "If you trust me and d
as I say, there will be no danger."

Tao frowned. "I do not understand."

The old man smiled weakly. "The longhorns hav
come back onto the high plains. Tomorrow is the da
of the hunt. Tonight we will paint images of th
great bulls on the walls of the Secret Cavern."

Tao was stunned. "But I am not a Chosen One. Th
elders will not accept me."

"I have trained you," said Graybeard, breathin
heavily. "And I will give the word so that the cla
people will know. You will make the spirits of th
longhorns live in the Secret Cavern."

"But you are still the Cave Painter."

"No, Tao, I can no longer lift my arms or hold
brush."

"Then you must rest and get well and you wil
paint again."

The old man bent over, coughing badly. "There i
no time. Even now the herds are on the high plain
The hunters are waiting."

"There are others."

"None as good as you. Your images are true and will please the spirits."

Tao shook his head. "It is a long journey."

"I can walk slowly."

"You are like an old boar," said the boy. "You will not give up."

"If you will not do this for me, I will try to do it myself."

Tao sighed and threw up his hands. "Then we must start now."

Graybeard spoke with the leader of the Mountain People again. They released Ram, and Tao was glad to see him safe and unharmed.

Still in a daze, with the sun still high in the sky, Tao helped the old man down through the spruce forest. They moved slowly, with Ram running on ahead, leading the way.

They came to the river, where Tao built a platform of willow branches and tied them together with vines. Graybeard sat crosslegged on the makeshift raft and the boy pushed it out into the stream. It bobbed and tossed on the current, sending up showers of cold water, drenching the old man. Tao winced as he saw Graybeard shivering with cold.

When they reached the far shore, the boy wanted to stop and build a fire, to let the old man rest and dry off.

But Graybeard shook his head, dragging himself along, his teeth chattering. "We must get there before dark," he said.

As Tao helped the old man along, his mind was filled with fear and doubt. All he knew now was that somehow, tonight, he would become a cave painter.

■ FIFTEEN

They walked slowly across the valley, with Graybeard leaning on Tao's shoulder, until they reached the foot of the limestone cliffs. Here Graybeard told Tao what to do. "Listen carefully," he said, "and do as I say."

Tao stood quietly, waiting for the old man to catch his breath. He could not believe this was really happening.

"Go up to the top of the cliffs, above the camp, and wait," said Graybeard. "As soon as darkness comes, climb down the narrow path to the entrance of Big Cave."

Graybeard took the deerskin bag from his shoulder. He reached in and pulled out a large seashell filled with tallow. In the center was a peat moss wick. The old shaman's hands trembled as he gave it to Tao. "Here is your lamp," he said. "Light it from the Endless Flame and begin your journey into the cave."

Even as Graybeard spoke, Tao could feel a cold chill creep up the back of his neck. He was not a Chosen One, yet he would go into the Secret Cavern. It was the greatest taboo of all.

But the old man brushed away Tao's doubts with a wave of his hand. "Follow the main tunnel until you come to the place where the passageway divides." Graybeard tapped the boy on the shoulder, on the same side as his lame foot. "Stay on this side and you will not go wrong. When you reach the Secret Cavern, it will be deserted. Begin your drawings of the great bulls at once."

Tao's mind was filled with a hundred questions. So much had happened in so short a time.

Graybeard leaned over, stifling a spasm of coughs. Then he straightened up and looked at Tao. Carefully, he draped the deerskin pouch over the boy's shoulder. "Here," he said, "this is yours now. Inside you will find the graven stones and all the other magic you will need."

Tao stepped back, stunned.

But Graybeard continued. "Draw and paint as many longhorns as you can. Then, when I come with the clan hunters, they will see how true your images are and they will know why I have chosen you as the new Cave Painter."

The old man stopped again. He was breathing hard and wheezing. "Go now," he said, "and remember what I have told you."

Tao watched the old man walk away. Slouched over, coughing badly, he disappeared into the dark oak wood forest.

Now the boy was alone with his thoughts and his doubts.

Tao left Ram in the little cave and told him to stay. Then he climbed up the cliffs and walked along the top until he was above the entrance to Big Cave. Below him the big fires blazed and he could see the camp of the clan people. He stayed in the shadows, sitting with his back against an old pine tree.

As he waited, he worried about Graybeard. He had never seen his old friend so thin and weak.

It seemed a long time before the sun set behind the purple mountains. The crickets began to chirp and a pair of nightjars called and swooped overhead.

Tao got up, his hands shaking, his legs unsteady. He curled his bad foot around his tree-limb crutch and started down the narrow ledge leading to Big Cave.

Far below he could see the clan hunters, tiny figures dancing around the big fire. Their chanting and singing drifted up to him on the damp night air. They were celebrating the coming hunt of the longhorns. Some of the men wore bison robes, their heads covered with antlers and horns. Bracelets of shells and bones around their legs and ankles jingled as they danced. Others wore masks carved in the images of bears or devils to ward off the evil spirits.

Tao moved cautiously, edging his way along, hiding behind the clumps of stunted evergreens growing out of the cliff side. Slowly he made his way closer, glad that the clan people were busy celebrating and would not see him.

He had just reached the cave entrance when suddenly he saw a young hunter climbing up the ledge to tend the Endless Flame. Quickly Tao moved back into the shadows, pressing himself against the cliff wall.

With dawdling slowness the young hunter performed his task. He threw armfuls of wood on the fire, sending up a shower of sparks that lit up the darkness. Tao held his breath. He was in plain view as he shrank back against the side of the white cliff. Yet neither the hunter nor the clan people below seemed to notice him.

As soon as the hunter was gone, Tao crept up and lit his tallow lamp from the Endless Flame. He took one last look around and started into the cave. He was familiar with the large room just within the entrance, for he had spent many winters here. It was empty now, and save for the flickering light coming from the Endless Flame it was gray and cold. Toward the back of the room was the entrance to the long, twisting passageway that led to the Secret Cavern.

Tao hesitated. He had never been beyond this point before and it gave him an eerie feeling to step past the opening. Holding his lamp high and limping along on his wooden crutch, he started down the dark tunnel. It was damp and gloomy, and his flickering lamp cast wavering shadows on the rough gray walls. Except for the occasional sound of dripping water, there was a cold stillness, like death.

Tao shuffled on, trying to hurry. He wanted to paint as many images as possible before Graybeard came in with the hunters. Soon the tunnel became narrower, with turns. Once, when the ceiling became too low, he got down on his hands and knees, pushing his lamp ahead of him.

Then, at an abrupt turn in the tunnel, Tao's heart jumped. A huge cave lion glared down at him. It swayed back and forth as he moved his lamp, and he realized he was looking at a lone painting done by an early cave painter on the wall of this hidden tunnel.

He continued on and soon came to the place where the passageway divided into two corridors. He stopped, undecided, and his heart sank. He could not remember which shoulder the shaman had touched. With a nagging doubt, he chose the one on the left.

A dank, musty odor filled the air, and the trickling sound of dripping water echoed throughout the tunnel. Slowly, Tao limped along, holding his lamp ahead of him. Then he stopped. He was sure he had taken the wrong turn.

Hurriedly he started back, almost running, stumbling in his haste, searching for the other path. He came to a second opening. Was this the one leading to the Secret Cavern? He wasn't sure. He felt a dampness in the palms of his hands. His heart was pounding furiously. More confused than ever, he started down the new tunnel.

He had only gone a short distance when a sharp hissing sound broke the silence and he was left in total darkness. A drop of water from the dripping ceiling had snuffed out his lamp.

For a long moment Tao stood petrified, numb with fear. He threw down the useless lamp and, with a trembling hand, began feeling his way along the damp walls. Totally blind, he groped through the blackness, not even sure that he was going in the right direction.

■ SIXTEEN

Tao limped on through the darkness, guided only by the unseen wall. The air was cool, yet he felt a dampness under his deerskin robe, and beads of sweat stood out on his forehead. He was trapped in this pitch-black underground passage. His hand brushed across the cold wall as he felt his way along, groping through the darkness with his left hand, holding tight to his crutch with the other. The gloom closed in on him, surrounding him, and he was sure he was going in the wrong direction. He shuffled along, slowly listening to the scraping of his feet, his eyes trying to penetrate the blackness.

Then he smelled the reeking odor of burning fat. It was faint, but he took a deep breath and it became stronger. He limped faster, his hand out in front of him, reaching. Smoke meant fire and fire meant light. He kept on going, his heart filled with new hope.

Suddenly, far in the distance, he thought he saw a faint glimmer of light. It danced for a moment, then went out. It came again, a pinpoint of brightness, far in the hazy darkness. It seemed to glow, then fade again. He limped toward it eagerly, stumbling, falling, then picking himself up.

The soft yellow gleam became brighter. The white haze and the burning smell became stronger. Tao was breathing fast, his heart beating wildly. Soon he was able to see clearly. He hurried on, almost running now. A few moments later he stumbled into a magnificent, brightly lit chamber.

Glowing tallow lamps were set in niches along the walls. Scattered across the floor of the cavern were hollowed-out stones and shells filled with paints and oils. Empty mammoth bones, standing upright, held brushes and sticks of charcoal. He blinked, and for a moment he looked around in silent awe, unable to believe his eyes. He had found the Secret Cavern.

Tao dropped his crutch and fell back against the wall, his mind filled with wonder. Many times he had heard about the Secret Cavern. But never did he imagine it held such splendor, such color and beauty.

Long rows of great hairy mammoths marched across the cavern wall, together with running horses, bristling boars and giant cave bears, all in varied shades of red, tawny browns and yellows. Images of woolly rhinos covered the opposite wall, while scattered groups of antelope and deer capered across the high, arched ceiling. The almost life-sized animals seemed to march through the cavern as if they were alive, moving and turning in the light of the flickering lamps.

Tao was amazed by the dazzling colors. The animals were just as he had seen them, as they wandered across the plains or through the forest. The roe deer were tense, the mammoths ponderous, the bears and cave lions strong and fearsome.

They were all here, brought to life in this secret place, the kind of drawings and images Tao had always dreamed of. He breathed deeply, filled with a sense of belonging. Now he would be a part of this secret place forever. He was glad that Graybeard had asked him to come.

Tao walked over to a large, unmarked portion of the wall. He rubbed across it with the palm of his hand and felt its cool, clean smoothness. He reached into Graybeard's leather pouch, his fingers groping around for the graven stones. One by one he took them out, until he found the slate with the engraving of the longhorn bull. He shook his hands to loosen them up, then picked up a large stick of charcoal. Now he would make his first mark on the wall of the Secret Cavern.

With a wide sweep of his arm he made a large outline.

He held up the sketch for a moment, studying it. Then he began to draw. He copied the sketch line for line, drawing the image of a longhorn.

He drew the great square head with its long, curving horns. He swung his arm freely, sketching in the massive shoulders, the thick chest and the muscular body. Next he reached into the deerskin pouch and took out a long flint chisel. Using a stone from the floor of the cave as a hammer, he began to carve out a shallow circle around the eye and nostril, just the way Graybeard had taught him.

For a moment he stepped back, nodding with satisfaction. Then, quickly, he outlined two, three, more longhorns, one behind the other.

With his bad foot he pushed three of the paint pots closer to the wall, where they would be within easy reach. He picked up a large feather brush and began filling in the colors, applying the yellows first, then shading in with reds and browns. Slowly the longhorns came alive, their muscles rippling, their sides heaving in the wavering lamplight.

On and on Tao painted, watching the herd of longhorns grow beneath his hand, watching it march across the long gray wall. He felt himself lifted up. He forgot about taboos. He forgot about the clan laws. He became so caught up with his painting that he even forgot about Graybeard and the clan hunters.

He finished his longhorns and now, with wild strokes of his brush, he outlined a mammoth, drawing the high-domed head, the curved tusks and waving trunk. He worked swiftly, with long, sweeping strokes, letting his hand flow freely over the cavern wall. Again he brushed in the colors, first the yellows, then the reds and browns and finally the deep shadows of black and gray.

He was almost finished when he heard the shuffling sound of feet coming through the tunnel. He turned slowly, the dripping paintbrush still in his hand. Now the hunters—Volt and Garth, all of them—would see how well he could draw, and Graybeard would name him the new Cave Painter. He stood quietly to one side, a proud smile on his face.

Tao watched as the clan hunters filed into the Secret Cavern. He saw them glance around, blinking in the flickering light. He waited for Graybeard to come in, but the old man was not with them. Suddenly Tao's smile died. He saw the look of horror on Garth's face and he knew he had done something wrong.

He heard a vengeful curse and turned to see Volt standing behind him, stunned disbelief burning in the big leader's eyes.

The hunters came toward him slowly, grumbling in their throats.

A cold sweat beaded his forehead. He held up his hand. "No," he pleaded. "No . . . Graybeard will tell you, it is the will of the spirits."

Volt stepped forward, pointing an accusing finger at the boy. His scarred face was contorted in livid rage. "You have defiled this secret place," he stormed. "You are a curse on this clan, you and that evil wolf dog." The violent words rang through the cavern and echoed in Tao's ears.

"Graybeard sent me here," Tao said, "to paint the longhorns." He pointed at the drawings he had just finished. "Graybeard."

But the hunters would not even look at the paintings. They crowded closer, glowering down at the boy.

"You lie," said Garth, pushing forward and pulling the leather bag from Tao's shoulder. He held it up for all to see. "Look, he has stolen the shaman's pouch."

"Perhaps he has killed Graybeard," said another, "and would now take his place."

Tao was stunned. He shook his head. "No," he said. "Graybeard gave me the pouch. He will tell you himself."

Volt's eyes narrowed. "Where is the shaman?"

Tao swallowed hard. "He did not come with you?"

"You know he is not with us," growled Garth. "What have you done with him?"

"Nothing," said Tao, his eyes begging them to understand. "Graybeard will come. He gave his word."

"Then where is he?" demanded Volt.

"I left the shaman near the oak wood. He was sick. But I would not harm him. He was my friend. He taught me to paint in the caves."

The hunters' eyes were filled with dark suspicion. They grabbed him roughly, pushing and pulling him through the twisting tunnel and out of the cave.

They took him down to the edge of the camp, where they bound his hands and feet.

In the dim light of the distant campfire Tao saw the fury in their eyes. "Find the shaman," he pleaded. "He will tell you I speak the truth."

Still the hunters would not listen. They gathered around him, bristling with anger, shaking their spears, their flint knives ready in their hands.

Just then Volt came into the light of the fire, his stocky legs planted wide apart, his eyes flashing. "Wait," he ordered. "The boy has angered the spirits of the longhorns. Now let him die by their wrath. Let him face Saxon, the sacred bull."

■ SEVENTEEN

His hands and feet tied with tough vegetable fibers, Tao lay on the damp ground under an oak tree. He looked off toward the big, rasping fire in the center of the camp and worried about Graybeard. He knew the clan hunters would be out searching for the old shaman, and as soon as they found him everything would be all right. The shaman will tell them he is too old to paint anymore, thought Tao, and he will name me the new Cave Painter. Because of the taboos, some of the hunters and elders will be displeased. But when Graybeard calls up the spirits they will accept it.

He was thinking of this when he saw four hunters carry a long burden wrapped in bearskins and set it on the ground near the big fire. At first he could not make out what it was. He saw some of the clan women kneel down beside it, their dark forms rocking back and forth. He heard them wailing and cry-ing and he realized it was a dead person.

Other women came. They uncovered the body and began smearing it with handfuls of red earth and clay. Then they wrapped it in birch bark in prepara-tion for burial.

Just then Tao heard a whimpering cry in the buck-thorn bushes behind him. He turned and saw a pair of yellow eyes staring at him from out of the darkness. With a sudden start, he knew it was Ram. "Go," he whispered. "Go away." He struggled against his binding, but he could not get free. He could not throw a stone or a stick. He whispered again, telling Ram to go, but the wolf dog did not move.

After the women had left he heard footsteps. Someone was coming to check his bindings. The footsteps came closer. Instantly the yellow eyes dis-appeared. The wolf dog had run off.

Tao waited, expecting one of the hunters. Instead in the dim light, he saw a woman standing over him. She leaned down and he recognized Kala.

The woman glanced around quickly, searching the darkness. She had a purselike object in her hand, holding it up by a long strap, and Tao saw that it was Graybeard's skin pouch.

Kala looped the strap over his shoulder, then tucked the pouch under his robe. "You told them Graybeard gave this to you," she whispered. "Then he would want you to keep it."

Tao felt a wave of hope. "They have found him?"

She put her finger to her lips. "Yes."

"Good," said Tao. "Now he will tell them of his promise."

Kala shook her head. "No, my son," she whispered. "The old shaman is dead. They found him lying in the oak wood."

Tao put his bound hands up to his forehead and closed his eyes as the words stabbed like a knife. "He was sick. I did not kill him. They must believe me. Graybeard was my friend."

"Hush," said Kala, her dark form leaning over him, a flint knife in her hand. "They will believe only the evil spirits. That is why I must cut you loose."

Tao pulled away. "No," he protested. "They would kill you for this."

Kala spoke under her breath. "I am an old woman. You have many summers yet."

Tao shook his head. "If I run away, they will be sure I have killed the shaman."

"And if you stay?"

"Then I will face Saxon." He spoke bravely, but deep inside he was afraid. "If I live, they will know I have spoken the truth. If I do not, then it does not matter."

Kala clicked her tongue and frowned. "You are like your mother. You are stubborn and you walk your own path."

The next morning the hunters untied Tao's feet and led him up the narrow ledge to the top of the cliff where the high plains began. Fear gripped him, but he would not let them see. He looked straight ahead, his lips tight.

They made him stand with his back to the edge of the cliffs. Far below was the wide green valley. In front of him, the high plains stretched away as far as he could see. Here, groups of longhorns and great herds of bison grazed peacefully on the vast waves of yellow grass.

In the distance Tao saw Saxon, the sacred bull. For more than eight summers the great beast had ruled over these stomping grounds. Now, standing in the bright sun, he seemed larger than ever, with his massive shoulders and long, sharp horns outlined against the horizon.

A cold chill crept up Tao's spine as, once again, he saw the bleached white bones of Saxon's victims scattered across the plains.

The hunters climbed to the top of a mound of rimrock, where they could watch the battle in safety.

Volt untied Tao's hands and gave him a spear. "It is the will of the spirits that you face Saxon with a weapon in your hands," he said.

Tao was thankful for the spear. It would help him keep his balance. He felt Graybeard's deerskin pouch hidden under his robe. He knew it contained only pieces of flint, the horn of a bison and some graven stones. Hardly the kind of magic that would stop a charging bull.

Volt walked over and climbed up on the rimrock

with the hunters. Garth and the others began waving their arms and jumping to attract Saxon's attention The big bull looked up, his great white horns gleaming in the bright sunlight.

The heavy muscles rippled under his shiny black hide as he trotted to the foot of the rock. He looked up, bellowing, glaring at the group of hunters.

Then he saw Tao standing alone, in the open within reach. For so large a beast he turned quickly With heavy strides he advanced, and now Tao could see the fire in his eyes.

Fighting back his terror, Tao stood rooted to the ground, his heart pounding wildly. He leaned on his spear, bracing himself, and waited for the attack.

The massive beast stopped directly in front of the boy, towering over him like an ominous shadow. His eyes blazed. His nostrils flared. Slowly he circled around, taking his time, eyeing Tao closely, as if he knew the boy could not escape.

Tao turned with him, standing on his good foot, balancing himself with his spear on the other.

Snorting and blowing, the black bull lowered his head and stabbed the ground with his horn. He pawed the dirt, kicking up clouds of dust. Then, with a bellowing roar, he charged.

Tao stood firm as the earth shook beneath him. He saw the long, sharp horns coming straight at him as the huge bulk of the animal filled his vision. At the last moment he threw himself to one side and rolled out of the way.

In a rage, the big bull tossed his head and whirled about, his splayed hooves trampling the dried grass.

Quickly Tao jumped to his feet, bracing himself for the next attack.

Once more Saxon lowered his head, flecks of white foam drooling from his mouth and nostrils. He tossed his head again and charged, boiling up clouds of dust.

Tao tensed, gritting his teeth, waiting for the right moment. Once again he sprang aside. But this time he felt a smashing blow as the bull's heavy shoulder slammed against his body, hurling him to the ground, knocking the spear from his hand. For a moment he lay dazed and shaken, unable to move.

Then, out of the corner of his eye, he saw Volt jump down from the rimrock, shouting and waving his arms. The enraged bull looked up, uncertain. It gave Tao time to scramble to his feet. But Saxon turned back quickly. Tao was his victim and he would not be distracted. Slowly he walked around the boy, dwarfing him in his shadow. With a wild rush he charged, hooves pounding, eyes blazing.

Tao dodged once more, just in time, as a long, curved horn caught the edge of his robe, spinning him around, throwing him to the ground. The deerskin pouch was torn free and dangled from his shoulder.

Chest and arms throbbing with pain, the boy looked up to see the bull turn, getting ready to charge again. Now there would be little chance to get out of the way. He fumbled blindly for his spear and desperately tried to gain his feet, but the great beast was coming fast.

Then, suddenly, he saw Graybeard's deerskin pouch lying at his side. Quickly he pulled it from his shoulder and swung it above his head. He whirled it around and around and let it fly just as the animal loomed over him. It struck the bull full in the face, the long strap tangling around its horns. Maddened and confused, Saxon ran off in a frenzy, tossing his head, strewing the contents of the bag over the ground.

Tao leaned on his spear, breathing heavily, trying to rest as the crazed beast ran around in circles. Saxon jumped and wheeled, thrashing about in an attempt to rid himself of the offensive object. Finally, with a toss of his head, the big bull sent the annoying bag flying into the grass. Now, more enraged than ever, Saxon turned, strings of foam dripping from his black lips. His nostrils flared and he lowered his head and charged.

Terrified, unable to move, Tao watched him advance. Then he saw a flash of sunlight flicker in the grass. He blinked and looked again. It was Graybeard's shining stone. With a wild leap he tumbled across the ground, scooping it up in his hand. He jumped to his feet and he turned it to the sun, shining the light directly in Saxon's eyes. The great bull slowed up. He stopped and shook his head, baffled and uncertain.

Grunting in fury, Saxon turned and charged again. Tao moved toward him, flashing the brilliant light across his face. Once again Saxon backed off. He trotted around in a wide circle, venting his anger with a bellowing roar.

Then he came back, head down, hooves pounding, shaking the earth. Again Tao caught the sunlight on the stone and flashed it in his eyes. The great bull wavered, then stopped as if facing a wall of fire. Trembling with rage, Saxon pawed the ground and jabbed his horns into the dirt. Tao followed him, forcing him back with the blinding light.

Frustrated, the bull swung his head from side to side, but Tao kept after him, giving him little chance to rest.

Finally the fire in his eyes was gone. His head drooped. Unable to understand this baffling brightness, the bull bellowed his vengeance to the sky. Panting heavily, his sides heaving, he tossed his head for the last time and left the field of battle. He trailed a cloud of dust across the plains as Tao saw him disappear into the distant herd of bison.

Volt walked over to Tao, followed by Garth and some of the hunters. The big leader shook his head in amazement. "No one has ever defeated Saxon before," he said. He waved his hand toward the hunters. "Yet the magic was here for all to see."

Tao's hands were shaking, his heart still pounding. He began picking up the graven stones, the amulets and the bison horn that had fallen out of

Graybeard's deerskin pouch. He started to tell Vol
there was no real magic. Then he remembere
Graybeard's voice. "If they wish to call it magic
then let it be so."

Volt paced up and down, shaking his spear. "It i
the will of the spirits," he said. "They have given th
sign and the word is good."

Tao stood quietly, trying to catch his breath as h
saw the rest of the hunters climb down from th
rimrock. Suddenly he heard a sound like muffle
thunder, rolling across the plains. It came from fa
off, in the direction Saxon had gone. A haze of dus
rose up all along the horizon as hundreds of grea
brown bodies came toward them like a gatherin
storm. It was a living wave of animals, growin
larger and larger, shaking the earth.

Volt's eyes grew wide with alarm. "Saxon ha
stampeded the bison," he shouted.

Even now Tao could see the host of panic-stricke
animals rushing toward them, heads bobbing up an
down, rows of curved horns flashing in the sunlight

"Run," shouted Volt. "Run!"

Garth and the hunters ran back, scrambling up th
face of the rimrock. Tao wrapped his bad foo
around the shaft of his spear and started after them
He gained the top of the rock just as the stampedin
herd reached the foot of the mound. The mass o
brown, shaggy bodies milled about below them
churning up clouds of dust. Choked and blinded, th
fear-crazed beasts ran about in circles, bawling
crashing into one another in a wild melee. Some o

he animals, crowded by the ones behind them, were
ushed over the edge of the cliff and fell to their
death on the rocks below.

Suddenly Tao's heart jumped. He did not remember Volt coming up the mound behind him. He
ooked around. The big leader was not on the
imrock, nor could he see him in the swirling dust
elow.

Moments passed before the rampaging herd began
o collect itself. It turned slowly and began walking
ack across the plains from where it had come. As he
urned, Tao saw a gray blur running across the
grass. "Ram!"

But as Tao started toward him, making his way
hrough the settling dust, he saw Volt, dazed and
haken, sitting on the ground beside the body of a
dead calf. And not far off was a lone cow bison. The
mother.

Quickly Tao started down the rock, jumping from
edge to ledge. He tried to hurry, but he was afraid
e would be too late. Halfway down he saw a gray
hadow leap from behind the rock and run with him.
t was Ram.

Growling and snapping, the wolf dog ran ahead,
arking at the shaggy beast, driving it back, as Volt
ot to his feet.

From the plain Tao came up shouting and twirling
he pouch. The bison turned, shaking her head, con-
used and uncertain. Reluctantly she stepped back,
hen turned and galloped off across the plains.

Tao rushed over to Ram. The wolf dog was slightly

gashed on the shoulder. Tao reached down and
pulled up handfuls of grass to stop the bleeding
Then he threw his arms around the panting animal

Volt's eyes held a wild, vacant stare as he gazed
toward the herd of bison now grazing peacefully in
the distance. He looked down at Ram, then raised
his hairy arms to the sky. "The curse is over!" h
shouted. "It has been lifted from my head. It is a
omen, a true sign from the spirits."

Tao sat on the ground, his arm around Ram'
shoulder. He knew Volt could never change. The de
mons and spirits would always rule his life.

"If I had not seen it with my own eyes," said Volt
"I would not believe it was so." He looked down a
Tao, a strange new expression on his face. "It is to
bad your mother does not live," he said. "She would
be happy now."

Tao turned, surprised by the unexpected words
"You knew my mother?"

Volt clasped his two fat hands together and hel
them up, making a big fist. "I knew your mother
when you were no bigger than that," he said.

Tao's dark eyes widened. With all his heart h
wished to know more. "What was she like?" h
asked.

Volt was silent for a moment, looking out across
the high plains, lost in his own thoughts. Then h
spoke. "She was a tall, fair woman," he said, "like
young birch tree. Yet she was strong and willful too
She saw things in a way the rest of us did not alway
understand."

Tao detected a twinge of guilt in the leader's voice, as if the words were hard to say.

The big man stared at the boy, studying him for a moment. Then he shrugged. "I will tell you no more," he said. "I will only say this: In many ways she was much like you."

It was the first time Tao ever heard Volt speak a quiet word. It was strange and unexpected. Yet it was the answer he had been seeking for so long.

He watched as the gruff leader walked away, and his heart pounded fiercely as he shouted the words, "You are my father!"

Volt turned, brushing his scarred cheek with the back of his hand. He glanced over his shoulder, a half smile on his lips as Garth and the other hunters came toward them. "You are a man now," he said. "You no longer need a father."

■ EIGHTEEN

They buried Graybeard in the little cavern high atop
the cliffs, overlooking the valley. Tao led the sad pro-
cession, with Ram walking by his side. He was
dressed in a new deerskin robe, a shiny necklace of
lions' teeth around his neck. Volt and the hunters
carried the old shaman's body lashed to a frame of
birch poles. The clan people followed close behind,
the children clapping sticks together, the women
wailing and crying.

They laid Graybeard in a shallow grave within the
little cavern. Tao placed a spear beside the body, together with a flint knife and a tallow lamp. Kala put
in portions of dried meat and nuts to help the old
one on his long journey to the land of the spirits. Finally they placed the shriveled body of a pygmy owl
in his hands as a token of his wisdom and knowl-
edge.

Tao stood at the foot of the open grave and looked around the cavern. He saw his paintings of the bison and the mountains-that-walk, and he remembered how often Graybeard had wagged his finger at him, making him do his drawings over and over again to make them better. He thought of the times they had spent together sharing salmon strips and roasting chestnuts. He thought of the long walks across the valley, through the Slough and along the shores of the big blue lake. He remembered all this and he felt a dull, aching emptiness in his heart.

They covered the grave with the rib bones of mammoths and threw on handfuls of earth and stones. After they filed out of the cavern, they rolled great boulders over the opening to block off the entrance from hyenas and wolverines.

Then, standing on the cliff overlooking the valley, Volt gathered the clan people around him. He held up Graybeard's amulets, his graven stones and bison horn, and gave them to Tao. "This day we accept Tao as our new Cave Painter," he said. "It is the wish of Graybeard and the will of the spirits."

Kala came forward with a new deerskin pouch. She placed it over Tao's shoulder, a proud smile on her wrinkled old face.

Tao reached out and touched her arm. Then he felt the dampness gathering in the corners of his eyes and he turned quickly. Together, he and Ram climbed down the cliff and into the valley. They walked across the verdant sea of waving grass, past the wandering herds of horses and antelope, and headed for the river. There they would cross over into the land of the Mountain People, where Tac knew he would have to prove himself again.

But he did not want to think of this just yet. For now he was following his dream. He was walking in Graybeard's footsteps.